Polly Samson was born in London in 1962 and spent most of her childhood in Cornwall and Devon. She has worked in publishing and as a journalist and has also written song lyrics. At 24 she was made a director of Jonathan Cape. Her features and reviews have appeared in, amongst others, the *Observer, Daily Mail* and the *Daily Telegraph* and for several years she wrote a column for the *Sunday Times*. She has published short stories in the *Observer* and the *Sunday Express* and on BBC Radio Four and BBC Radio Scotland. Virago will publish her first novel *Out of the Picture* in April 2000. She lives in Sussex with her husband and their three young sons.

Lying in Bed

Polly Samson

A *Virago* Book

Published by Virago Press 2000
First published by Virago Press 1999

A CIP catalogue record for this book is
available from the British Library

ISBN 1 86049 667 9

Typeset in Bembo by M Rules
Printed and bound in Great Britain by
Clays Ltd, St Ives plc

Virago Press
A Division of
Little, Brown and Company (UK)
Brettenham House
Lancaster Place
London WC2E 7EN

Contents

For David

Wasted   Time

She had long since stopped looking into her father's eyes for a twinkle. That was for kids. She knew precisely where babies came from, how they were made and even how they were prevented from being made. Her mother had fooled her when she *was* still a kid, wasted so much of her time, with the oft-repeated: 'This all happened when you were just a twinkle in your father's eye,' when she reminisced about her glory days protesting outside the American Embassy or about the terror of the air raids in London, for example. The girl felt foolish whenever she remembered how she used to frame her father's face in her stubby hands, searching his eyes, longing for that elusive twinkle and the baby brother or sister it would bring.

Her fury when all this twinkle stuff was revealed as nonsense had strengthened her mother's resolve to be

3

honest with her daughter, so she took her into her bed and explained the facts of life, peppering her account of conception with the word love:

'When a mummy and daddy love each other they cuddle in bed at night.'

'Yes, I know.'

'Well, sometimes they love each other so much that they want to get even closer and, well . . .'

'Yes?'

'Well, then the daddy puts his willy inside the mummy's special place. It's called making love and sometimes it makes a baby.'

'But how does *that* make a baby?' asked the girl, enjoying the combination of her mother's discomfort and the warmth of her body.

Not for the first time, the girl's mother found herself wishing that the job of parenting were more equally shared with her husband. With a deep sigh she explained about sperm ('love seeds', she said) and eggs while her daughter looked doubtful. 'That's how a baby is made,' she said, finally.

'Honest truth?' said the girl, and her mother held out her hands to show that her fingers were not crossed.

'Honest truth,' she said. 'That is how *you* were made.'

The girl snuggled closer, savouring the familiar warm, carroty smell of her mother's skin.

'Do you and Daddy ever make love?' she asked.

Her mother laughed, squeezed her tighter.

'Oh yes, often,' she said.

Now this was all very well, thought the girl, but if they made love often as her mother claimed, then why did she not have brothers and sisters. It was all highly suspicious, just like that 'twinkle in your father's eye' stuff before. Resigned and embarrassed, her mother explained about condoms and then suggested that the girl should help her shell peas in the kitchen.

A few months later, the girl discovered her father's condoms. She hadn't been looking for them but was rifling through his bedside cupboard in search of the bitter chocolate German biscuits that he sometimes hid there. On previous raids, she had noticed the sky-blue conical tin but her panic about the biscuits had prevented her from looking inside. But on this day, she had time to survey all the contents of his cupboard while her parents were digging potatoes in the vegetable garden. She could see them there out of the window, backs bent, as she leafed through a stack of old sepia photographs (all very boring, mainly of children she didn't recognise in starchy-looking overalls playing in a garden). There was a passport, some playing cards and some bottles of pills. Her parents were still digging. She unscrewed the top of the blue tin and found inside five identical foil wrappers of the same shade of blue. 'Durex Elite Condoms' was printed on each.

This discovery set the girl on an obsessive daily ritual. Without fail, when she returned from school, she would sneak into her parents' bedroom and count the foil packages. She didn't have a clue what 'often' meant but she knew that if the numbers decreased then her parents still loved each other and would not get divorced as she so often heard her mother threatening, her fiery rage not taking account of the terrified child in the next room. Once, about a year after the ritualistic stock control started, there had been six condoms there for sixteen days. She became morose and jumpy. She plagued her mother, asking her, again and again, 'You do still love Daddy, don't you?' until one of the sky-blue packages was, at last, missing.

When the school Easter holidays started, the girl discovered that she could not get on with her day until she had found a moment's peace to count her father's condoms. She would linger over French toast, watching her mother reading the *Guardian*; turning the pages and sighing, as though the whole world were her family, and each piece of bad news a personal bereavement. She knew that as soon as her mother finished reading the news, she would take her coffee and settle with the crossword, a pencil and the dictionary in a fat black chair in the sitting room. She hated to be interrupted while she was working at this and the girl was happy to oblige, taking the opportunity to check up on her parents' love life.

The house where they lived was a former vicarage built of thick grey granite slabs and nine miles from the nearest town. It was rare that other children would be invited to play – her mother disliked small talk and therefore most of her schoolfriends' parents too, describing them to her husband as 'petit bourgeois'. In any case she was too busy for children's tea parties, what with the crossword and writing her book in the afternoons. The girl was busy too.

Each day, once she had counted the condoms, she had her market stall to attend to. Next to the vicarage was a small paddock, full of the sort of things that passers-by might need. The girl would take empty yoghurt pots, silver foil, old colour supplements, scraps of Christmas wrapping paper, sellotape, scissors and needle and thread into the paddock. She bound together elaborate arrangements of primroses, sorrel and laurel leaves, placing them into the pots, which she covered with silver foil. Then she would scout along the Cornish hedges looking for the elusive miniature violets that grew beyond the bushes of hawthorn and gorse. These she would sew neatly on to the yoghurt pots, alternating them with daisies when she couldn't find enough violets. From gnarled rhododendron twigs she made frames for the pictures of horses, dogs and babies that she cut carefully from the magazines. She filled old shampoo bottles with water and added the coconut-scented yellow buds of gorse and tiny blue eyebrights.

These treasures she would take to the milk churn stand of the disused dairy along the lane. Each item would be neatly labelled with its price and she would arrange and rearrange them as she sat on the cold stone stand, waiting. It was the remoteness of the Old Vicarage that had attracted her parents to it in the first place; the closure of the tin mines in the previous century had more or less sounded the death knell for the entire village. There was no reason for anyone to pass by and the girl would soon move on to her next activity of the day. This was lying in the middle of the road with her eyes shut, imagining a car speeding along the

7

tiny lane and the excitement of having to jump out of its way. Once she slept there for over two hours.

After her picnic lunch – usually peanut butter sand-wiches and lemon barley water, which she prepared for herself as her mother didn't eat in the daytime – she had her visiting to do.

Charles, Henry and Lucy lived next door. Actually they didn't live. Next door was the Victorian churchyard. Only a churchyard, now disused and without a church since it had been burned down in unexplained circum-stances after the congregation dwindled to such an extent that the church was deconsecrated. The last vicar commit-ted suicide. When the police arrived, they found him in a pool of his own blood, both wrists cut from the heel of his hands to his elbows, his wife beside him, knitting. It was said that you could still hear the clack of her needles in the vicarage on the anniversary of his death; the girl marked the date on her wardrobe door.

Charles and Lucy were brother and sister. Their head-stones were simple granite slabs, covered in moss. Lichen clung to the carved inscriptions of their names and dates. Charles Bolitho 1822–1828 (he was six) and Lucy Bolitho 1823–1831 (she was eight). All the graves were unattended; docks and nettles ran wild; many of the headstones were crumbling. The girl had been drawn to Charles and Lucy when she was chasing a Red Admiral butterfly the summer before. The grass was up to her knees and she almost tripped over Lucy's headstone. Later the same day, she dis-covered Henry's grave. He was often her favourite of the three children. Henry's headstone was also of granite but was carved into a cross. It, too, was overgrown but she had picked away at the moss with the buckle of her sandal and discovered that Henry Worsfold was only four and had been born in 1819. She wished that she could move Henry closer to Charles and Lucy. She knew that he was lonely and wanted someone to play with.

As no one ever called by to buy her primroses and violets, the girl would share them, dividing them fairly between the three children. Henry was the only one who liked peanut butter, so she made honey sandwiches for Charles and Lucy. She wished that her father had more chocolate biscuits because then she could take some for them, too. But he would notice if she took four each time she raided the packet, so she brought them the plain digestives that her mother used for making lemon cheesecake and didn't mention the chocolate biscuits for fear of making them jealous. Sometimes she brought a book and read to them, but mostly she sat quietly. When her parents had a particularly violent row, which was about once a month, she would find solace in telling Lucy and Charles about it; but she kept the details from Henry, who was too young to understand. One of the two nicest things that happened during the holiday was when she found a small, perfect blackbird's egg on Charles' grave. It was a delicate blue, speckled with dark brown.

The other thing that most pleased her that Easter happened just two days after the blackbird egg. A baby jackdaw, small as a budgerigar, had fallen from its nest in the beech tree that shadowed Henry's grave. The girl found it, flapping one wing hopelessly in a tangle of grass, its black beak opening and shutting, its visible eye piercing her. She wrapped it in her cardigan and ran with it to her mother's study. 'You may keep it, if you must, but it won't live,' warned her mother. 'The kindest thing you can do is put it out of its misery now.'

The girl would not countenance such a murder and felt sure that she could nurture the jackdaw. After all, it already had a name: Jackanory was what she decided on while still running from the churchyard.

She made a nest for the baby jackdaw with the broken wing in one of the kitchen drawers. She padded the nest with an old grey bath towel and put a saucer of water by its beak. She didn't much like worms but she dug in the vegetable garden until she found some small enough to handle and tried to tempt the jackdaw, with a pair of chopsticks substituting for its mother's beak. It neither ate nor drank. In fact it did very little except try to peck her whenever she lifted it up to inspect its wing or change its lying position. When her father returned from work, late and flustered, he agreed that it would be kinder to wring its neck.

Supper that night was an uncomfortable affair. Her mother slammed dishes on the table, her father left the casserole mostly untouched. The girl could feel a familiar, ominous blackness sweeping over her mother. She hoped it wasn't her fault, she hoped it wasn't because she had insisted on keeping the jackdaw. Most of all, she hoped that there wasn't going to be an explosion. She hated that more than anything. She couldn't bear seeing her mother lose control. It always felt so dangerous.

At bedtime, she tried to cheer herself up by drinking hot chocolate from the delicate porcelain cup that had contained her Easter egg. All the other mugs in the house were ancient stoneware, brown and chipped. This one was white and decorated with pink roses. She went to bed early and lay there, terrified, singing to herself from *The Sound of Music*.

The row started soon after, building from a low rumble in the kitchen to the predictable crescendo of her mother's screams. It was one of the bad ones and soon the girl could hear the smashing of crockery. Involuntarily, her foot started beating a tattoo against the mattress, like a rabbit in terror. Pat pat pat pat pat. A steady beat as the shouting and destruction carried on below. Suddenly she remembered her Easter cup. She had left it on the table.

With her heart pounding, she crept to the bottom of the stairs and peered through the crack in the kitchen door. The crashes were regular now, filling the pauses between her mother's venomous words:

'I . . . *crash* . . . have . . . *crash* . . . had . . . *crash* . . . enough . . . of . . . you . . . *crash* . . . Do something . . . You . . . think . . . I should . . . *crash* . . . be . . . *crash* . . . happy . . . Never . . . *crash* . . . *crash* . . . *crash* . . .'

She was standing by the open cupboards where the crockery was stacked. The girl's father was surrounded by broken shards, his arms raised around his head protectively, crouching by the washing machine and trying to make himself heard above the furore. The girl could see her treasured china cup on the kitchen table. Her mother was still screaming as she reached again inside the cupboard. Nothing. She knew what her mother would do. When it happened it was like an action replay. As the hysterical woman reached for the Easter cup, the girl shot through the door, screaming, 'No!' But her mother's hand was already there, her motor responses too tuned to this orgy of destruction to be able to stop. Her eyes met her daughter's as she hurled it through the air. In the same movement she swept the girl into her arms and fled, eyes streaming, from the room.

She rocked her sobbing daughter in her arms. Told her how sorry she was, clinging, while the girl struggled to free herself, speechless. She left her mother sitting uselessly in the big black chair and went to the kitchen. She already knew that the jackdaw would be dead. Dead from shock. An insignificant death, they would tell her, but just the same, the girl felt that she could have prevented it. When she retrieved the bird from the war zone of the kitchen, its eyes were shut. Terrified that her mother would return to the scene of the crime, she picked up the whole drawer and took it to her room. She fashioned a coffin from a shoe box, lining it with a soft woollen vest, and placed Jackanory inside.

The next morning she got up early. Her father was still asleep on the sofa. Her mother had cleared up the kitchen and was sitting, eyes ringed with black, at the table. She didn't look up as her daughter headed with the shoe box and the fire shovel for the paddock. By the paddock gate there was a small grassy mound where the girl's favourite primroses grew. Instead of plain yellow with greenish centres, these ones were stained blood red, the centres almost black. The girl carefully removed a square of turf covered in the crimson primroses, and set it aside. She dug a hole big enough for Jackanory and his shoe-box coffin. She found a flat rock to mark his grave and placed the box inside. Then she started replacing the earth. All that was left to cover was the tiny jackdaw's head. He opened one eye, the membranous lid revealing its blue cracked-china iris. Resolute, in need of a funeral, the girl continued shovelling earth, until nothing more could be seen of the jackdaw. Carefully she replaced the primrosed turf, stuck in the headstone and wrote his name on the rough granite surface in black crayon. Then she returned to the house.

Without hesitation she went to her parents' bedroom. She opened her father's bedside cupboard, found the sky-blue tin. Inside were three foil-wrapped condoms. From the waistband of her jeans she drew a fine sewing needle. She pierced the first condom through the packet, 'Charles,' she whispered, and then the second, 'Lucy,' and the third, 'Henry.'

Moss Roses

I was at my piano playing Beethoven, or it might have been Elton John. Maybe it was Elton John because I was thinking about Fiona and, to be quite honest, brushing up on 'Your Song', which has quite a tricky middle section. 'Your Song', which was our song, to play for Fiona that evening. Casually, of course.

I don't often play the piano these days, I don't know why; but Fiona likes it when I do and I like to please her. She is so impressed by these things. A bit of Brahms, the 'Moonlight Sonata', 'Clair de Lune', 'Air on a G String', all the old favourites. I swear she gets a tear in her eye when I play! Such a sweet girl!

She likes it here at Harlington, and I am rejuvenated by seeing it all through her eyes. I see the enthusiasm, or dare I say the *adoration*, of a beautiful young girl as a bit of a reward for the generations of work that my ancestors and I have put into the place.

Harlington: so much to do and barely a moment to call my own. A man should feel at peace in his house, it's a basic human need. But it's so hard for me here, forever tripping over estate workers, worse still, the children of estate workers, trespassing over the park, snotty-nosed, obviously up to no good in their muddy trainers and garish sweatshirts. I can't go for a walk without someone wanting something: the old oak by the front lodge has suffered in the storm, should we call in the tree surgeon? How many beaters do we need for the weekend pheasant shoot? Old Simpkin's roof still leaks, should we agree to having it releaded or just patched up again? Would I like an early crop of pink fir apples again this year?

'Yes,' I say, and, 'The usual dozen lads, of course,' and, 'Have you had any quotations for the work? Yes, you have? Well this should go through the estate office,' and, 'Please speak to the kitchen staff and not me about this.'

Sometimes I feel there is no escape. I can leave the grounds and head for the house. There are flowers and pictures and rugs and drapes: renovation, cleaning, replacing. It's endless. Harlington needs a woman's touch again. My wife used to manage all that, you see, she had the house running tickety-boo, but that was before she turned to smoking the white stuff with the black boys in London. She's long gone and I feel nothing but relief.

I sit at my piano and play. Outside I can see the gardens stretching before me, and the parkland beyond. The lawns are thickly planted with deep purple crocuses but there is little other colour at this time of year. Still, Simpkin, the old head gardener, is out there, familiar as any of the statuary. He is stooped over his rose bushes, clipping away at the old wood and coughing into his handkerchief. I am trying to play the piano but Simpkin distracts, snip-snipping and coughing just a few feet from me, the other side of the window pane. He makes me uncomfortable, so much so that I move away, irritated by the industrious, slow labour of the man.

I walk to the morning room, away from the piano and Simpkin. Joan brings me my pot of tea and kneels at the hearth to poke the fire, to put on another log.

'I heard you playing just now,' she says. 'It were so beautiful, it quite reminded me of when you were a boy.'

Joan was my nanny then and I have kept her on as housekeeper. She's a dear old thing who knows me and my funny ways. No one makes a Queen of Puddings quite like Joan.

'I remember when her ladyship would let you play that piano sitting on her lap when you were no more than three. You had an ear for music, even then,' she says.

They used to tell me that if I played enough, practised more perhaps, I would make concert standard, but the house has always taken so much of my time. Estate matters must come first.

Fiona will arrive this evening. She will be on the 8.32 from Paddington. She will bring with her the stench of the city. Lovely though she is, I prefer not to touch her until she has soaked in the bath. I will leave her up to her neck in Crabtree and Evelyn to calm down a bit, stop chattering in the neurotic, high-octane tones of the London career girl. The last thing I need is a headache on a Friday evening.

Perhaps I will take her out to the orangery again after dinner. I can see her now, spread-eagled on the marble tiles, alabaster naked among the woody roots of muscat, as I stand above her viewing her by the light of a single candle. Watching her wide brown eyes as she tries to hold my gaze, I revel in her shyness. I think of her frozen like a rabbit caught in a searchlight. That's how I like her: exposed, silent and a little bit frightened.

I take my teacup and stand at the terrace doors, looking out across the lawns to the orangery. There is some music playing on the wireless, Elgar, I think, pleasant enough. It is raining now and I can see Simpkin again through the steamy glass as hc darts his secateurs in and out of the thorny dormant skeletons of the moss roses that were planted for my grandmother. He is bent over his work, kneeling now on the wet earth, collecting the twisted dead wood into a green tarpaulin, water streaming from the shoulders of his blackened oily jacket, splashing from the brim of his brown felt hat and on to his muddied bare hands. The backdrop of the orangery looms out of the rain, streaks of grey and celadon, its glass and ironwork dissolving before my eyes like a watercolour. Simpkin concertinas back on to his haunches, coughs into his sopping handkerchief again. Why won't the man shelter? He really is making me uneasy. I feel haunted by the spectre of the silly old fool.

Joan finds me at the doors watching Simpkin. 'That man,' she sighs, 'he shouldn't be out there in his condition. It's his chest. I keep telling him to get Jack and Henry out there when it's like this, but he won't listen to a word.'

'He's a foolish old man,' I say.

'And not long for this world, if he keeps this up,' says Joan. 'Dr Beale told me that one more bout of pneumonia and he'd be dead for sure. But he's obsessed by them moss roses. I think he only lives to see them flower once more. He talks to them, you know, I swear it's true, I heard him.' Joan talks while she fusses at my tray, refreshing the tea and rearranging the ginger biscuits on the plate.

I am not a sentimental man but I can stand the spectacle of old Simpkin out there for not a moment longer. 'For goodness' sake,' I say, 'do tell the old dolt to step in here. I want to talk to him. I can't abide the soggy sight of him out there for another second.'

I watch, moments later, as Joan crosses the lawn, stoutly marching beneath her red umbrella. Simpkin stands, stiffly unfolding hinges, but never quite upright, and wipes his hands on his mossy old moleskins. I see him look up at the house, a shrug, talking to Joan and then back to the house again. I open the doors to the rain-soaked terrace and gesture to him to hurry on in. Simpkin folds his secateurs, pockets them, and moves slowly across the lawn, reluctant as my old labrador, feet heavy as clay, following Joan.

I stand at the terrace doors. 'Simpkin,' I say, 'please step in here where it's warm.'

Simpkin stops when he gets to the terrace, water running from his clothes. 'Sir, I'm too filthy wet, I will muddy your floor if I come further,' he says.

'Just step in, never mind the mess,' I say. 'Quickly now, I'm getting cold.'

Simpkin stands before me, just inside the morning room doors, staring at his boots and the muddy water that is collecting around them. He holds his brown felt hat in his hands. I will ask him to plant some new roses just for Fiona, I think, somewhere in the rosebeds outside the orangery, my night garden of delight. I would like her to take an interest in the gardens. My mother once did an excellent course at the Chelsea Physic Gardens. I will tell dear Fiona all about it and that I invited poor old Simpkin in for tea.

'Joan,' I say, 'get the man a towel. And a teacup. You will take a cup of tea, Simpkin?'

Simpkin stoops over his boots, large, gnarled fingers, skin roughened as bark, struggling with the wet, knotty laces. His coat is already steaming and water drips from his hair. He smells of wet peat and sawdust; not too bad, really.

Joan takes Simpkin's oilskin and hat from him to dry them in the kitchen. I hear her tut-tut as I invite Simpkin to sit by the fire, and she spreads the maroon dog blanket over one of the fireside chairs. She does not approve of estate workers being invited into the big house; it just doesn't happen.

Simpkin sits on the edge of the chair, wiping his hands on a corner of the towel, shifting his feet, self-consciously twisting them behind the chair legs, attempting to conceal his socks, grey wool stained brown from the combination of rain and dubbin.

'You wanted to speak to me, sir? I trust everything in the garden is as you would like it?' Simpkin stares into the fire, unaware that his right hand moves gently, minutely conducting the Elgar, forefinger resting lightly on his thumb, an involuntary baton held there.

'Yes,' I reassure him, 'the garden is as it should be for the time of year. I was just considering replacing one or two of the moss roses nearest the orangery.'

Simpkin looks up, sharply, as though I have insulted him. 'Oh no, sir, you don't want to be doing that. They are beauties, every one of them. They flower their little hearts out. Just once, mind, not like those awful new roses that keep going. But the blooms. I ain't never seen blooms like them before or since. And so much moss on each bud, they get quite curled some, and then the flowers burst through, unfolding their petals, pushing all that moss aside. Like a birth, every one of them. Petals of blood and wine. You'll never see anything more beautiful than that in a garden. And the perfume! You have noticed the perfume?' Simpkin's eyes are shining.

'Thank you, Simpkin,' I say, astounded. 'If you think they are not too old and woody, I will trust your judgement. But I would like to add some new bushes for Fiona, in the beds closest to the orangery.' I had been vaguely thinking about long-stemmed white roses, white as her swan's throat, but now I think about what Simpkin said, and remember the moss roses. How my mother loved those roses! I think about the moment before flowering, when each plump fuzzy amber bud splits open at the tip to reveal the soft pink folding petals inside. So erotic! So very Fiona.

Simpkin looks more relaxed, he is back to the music, his head and his hand perceptibly swaying to the sound of a lone violin. He hasn't touched his tea and I gesture to him to drink it. The duck-egg-blue bone china looks too delicate in his knotty, oak tree hand, as though the handle might snap. It rattles as he replaces it on the saucer.

'I'll get you a rose catalogue, if you'd like. Hawkins' catalogue has many good mosses, on good sturdy root stock too, that'll flower this summer, if we get them right. I will get them right for you, sir. They'll be covered in blooms by June.' Now that the tea is finished, Simpkin leans back against the dog blanket, happy to be talking about his beloved roses. I am refreshed by his enthusiasm.

'That would be most helpful. I can see that you are a fan of Elgar,' I add, watching his hands as they count in the next movement of the music.

'Ah yes, Opus Twelve, "Salut d'amour", it's a favourite of mine,' he says, astonishing me once again.

We talk about music for a while. 'You might be able to help me,' he says, momentarily forgetting about his socks and stretching his feet towards the fire. 'There's a piece of music that I've been trying to trace for years and I can't find

it anywhere. Have you heard of Galos? That's the composer, but I don't know anything more than that, just this
one composition that I heard when I was a young lad. It's
a beautiful piece, "Le Lac de Come". It would bring tears
to the eyes of a statue.' He is as ardent about his music as
the roses. I find that I stop pitying him after a while, and
welcome the interruption to the routine ennui of a wet
Friday at Harlington.

Fiona likes to walk in the gardens after Sunday lunch,
before she heads back to London, to what she calls her real
life. Harlington is like a dream to her. We wander through
wild garlic, our boots imprinting a pungent trail of crushed
wet leaves, and she says that she feels like Alice stepping
through the looking-glass when she passes through the
front gates each Friday. 'It's like time travel,' she says. 'I
arrive in another century.' I laugh. I tell her that when she
leaves we are frozen like in a game of musical statues, that
we only come back to life when she returns.

'Yes, you're all carved out of stone,' she says. 'I mean,
just look at him.'

She is pointing at Simpkin, bowed beneath his brown
felt hat, working at the orchard wall, knotting thick green
twine which loops from one of the bulging pockets of his
earth-encrusted canvas smock, tying back the wayward
branches of espaliered nectarines, and whistling.

'Look at your Simpkin,' she says. 'There's no way he's
real. He's older than the Queen Mother. Gardeners only
look like that in costume dramas.'

Simpkin looks up and touches his hat as we approach.

'Afternoon, Simpkin,' I say. 'Better weather today.'

'Do you know, sir, and miss,' he says, easing his hands into the small of his back, attempting to straighten himself for Fiona, 'there are already daisies on the lawns. It's that mild. Daisies in February. The world is topsy-turvy. I've worked these gardens since I was a boy and we've never seen daisies in February, not in seventy years we haven't.'

'It's the greenhouse effect,' says Fiona. 'The earth's heating up, isn't that right?'

'Well, whatever it is, it's not as it should be,' says Simpkin.

He reaches into one of his pockets and produces a crumpled coloured pamphlet.

'This is the Hawkins' catalogue I mentioned, for the roses you wanted,' he says, unfolding it then wiping the cover across his sleeve, before handing it to me. 'I've turned down the corners of the pages that'll interest you. The moss roses.'

'Thank you, Simpkin,' I say. 'Fiona and I will choose some roses over tea. Perhaps you would call by the kitchens later and I will ask Joan to let you know which ones we have selected.'

'Very good, sir,' says Simpkin. 'We'll need to get started with them as soon as we can if they're to settle in before the weather heats right up. They'll be happy to bloom for us by the summer if we get them in and comfortable soon.'

'Settled in?' says Fiona, as we head back to the house.

'Comfortable? He's obviously quite batty. He talks about rose bushes as though they're children.'

'He's a man of surprising passions,' I say. 'You should hear him on music. You remember I was telling you about when he came in, out of the rain, for tea the other day? Well, I could barely get rid of him. He had me on a wild-goose chase, going right through the *Grove Dictionary of Music* looking for some piece or other that he has been trying to trace for years. Well, Grove doesn't even have a listing for the composer, so you're probably right, he is batty. He's even written to the BBC to see if they have a recording, which, of course, they haven't. But nevertheless, quite marvellous for an old man of the soil, don't you think?'

'Nothing surprises me, here,' says Fiona. 'After all, it is Wonderland.'

But Simpkin, it turns out, is not as deluded as we thought. When Fiona has gone, Joan brings me my hot milk along with some sheet music that Simpkin dropped off when he collected the rose catalogue from the kitchens. It is 'Le Lac de Come' by Galos, the music that the old boy has been looking for. 'I think he wants it for his funeral,' says Joan, 'and that's not far off.'

I take the crumpled sheet music into the music room and sit at my piano. My lazy fingers struggle to find the notes, at first, and then I become absorbed. The piece starts with a slow, low arpeggio. As my right hand moves to the keyboard, the phrase changes, the melody arrives in broken chords, emulating a harp. Then quickly played repeating

notes that sound like a mandolin. It is haunting, sentimental, unquestionably romantic, like the theme music for an
Italian film, a pre-First World War love story, perhaps. Was
Simpkin ever in love? I find myself wondering. Since I was
a boy, he has been in the gardens. He has been old for as
long as I can remember.

'You should record it for him,' says Fiona, when I
play her Simpkin's music. 'You play it so beautifully.' But
what with estate matters and taking Fiona to hear Pavarotti
sing at the Holders House opera festival in Barbados over
Easter, several months pass before I so much as touch the
piano again.

The roses I chose for Fiona are planted by the
orangery in two new circular rosebeds. They have been
rooted in and nurtured by Simpkin, who dug the holes and
filled them with his own secret-recipe compost. 'There,
you'll be comfortable here now,' he tells them. 'You will
have the best start when you reach down with your roots
and find all those lovely nutrients.' He has tended them
well. The base of each plant he has covered with bonemeal
and protected with a thatch of golden wheat straw, pressed
right into the bole, from which the budding, furred
branches stick up like antlers.

When I take Fiona to see her rose bushes – 'See how
much I love you?' I say. 'I promised you a rose garden, and
here it is!' – she looks doubtfully at the bare branches and
then reminds me again that I should record 'Le Lac de
Come' for Simpkin. 'How would you feel if he died and
you hadn't done that one simple thing?' she asks. 'Yes, yes,'

I say, steering her towards the orangery doors. 'You're right.
I should do it.'

Fiona has been around long enough to start bossing
me about and I'm not sure I like it. 'Tonight,' she says,
stopping me in my tracks and flicking what I hope is imaginary dust from the shoulders of my blazer, 'you will
record it tonight. Then it's done.'

I remind her that my old friend Hugo and his wife
Belinda are staying for the weekend. 'I'm quite sure that
they don't want to hear some silly little piano piece,' I say.
What does she want me to tell them, that I have to record
it for the *gardener*?

Women. They always get their way. After a good
dinner of quail with Joan's spectacular game chips, I, for
one, wanted to take my Armagnac into the library. Quite
how I found myself in the music room, seated obediently at
the piano, with Hugo and Belinda looking bemused and
Fiona setting up a little microphone from the tape recorder,
I do not know.

'Just play something, anything,' she says, as she tests
the machine, repositioning the microphone on a pile of
books. 'Old boy,' says Hugo, pursing his lips in studied
amusement, 'a little music after dinner, how charming.'

I start to play the Galos but it has been a long time
and it takes me several goes. Hugo enjoys fine wine and
with his encouragement I have had rather more than my
usual few glasses of claret at dinner. 'Stop a moment,' says
Fiona. 'I just need to test the machine.' Hugo helps himself
to another Armagnac while Fiona rewinds the tape and

plays back the opening chords. It sounds clear enough to me, and she is satisfied that it will be good enough for Simpkin. 'OK,' she says, giggling now, 'from the top.'

I am starting to enjoy the attention as Hugo's ravishing wife Belinda stands beside me in her silver sequins, watching my fingers as they crawl up and down the keyboard. 'Hah! She's hypnotised!' I think, as she moves closer, leaning her body, pressing it into the side of the piano.

'Oh bugger!' I say, as I miss a note. Fiona jumps and switches off the machine. 'That was so beautiful, I love the piano,' says Belinda. 'What is it?' I explain about Simpkin, about his passion for this piece, how he cannot trace a recording, and with a signal from Fiona, start to play again as she presses the record button. I get to the end of the piece with a flourish and smile at Belinda. 'There,' I say, 'I've done it. Fiona can stop pestering me now and the old fool can pop his clogs and have this at his funeral.' I reach for my glass and raise it in the air. 'To Simpkin.'

'To Simpkin!' exclaim the others and we all toast the old man and collapse into fits of giggles at the bizarre prospect of my going to all this trouble for one of my gardeners.

I wander in the grounds a lot at this time of year but Simpkin is nowhere to be found. I love the early summer in the garden. My mother, God rest her soul, used to walk with me and tell me the names of the plants. Thus I know that the tall, staked spires of shivering intense blue are delphiniums, that the bushes that look as though they are studded with bright pink and cream and maroon paper butterflies are the cistus and the large shrubs around the fountains that are hung with lacy white pompoms are viburnum opulis. I know too about the moss roses. The rose bushes that I planted for Fiona are covered in downy buds; they will flower in the next few weeks. As the days go by, and I see no sign of Simpkin in the garden, I find myself haunting the rose gardens with the tape of Galos in my pocket.

'He's been taken so bad,' says Joan when, finally, I ask about Simpkin, 'he's been in the hospital all week, on a ventilator and everything, but he's home now. Apparently, he just walked out. The nurses were very upset.'

'Would he be well enough to take tea with me?' I find myself asking.

'I could find out, if that's what you would like. I could go up to the gardener's lodge now. Between ourselves, I think he's only come back to see the roses.'

'Yes,' I say, 'perhaps you would tell him that I would like to see him here. I should insist that he gets proper medical attention. After all, he has served my family well.' But then I think about old Simpkin, struggling across the park. Maybe he'd die on the way, or collapse in front of me in one of my chairs.

'No,' I say, 'forget tea. I'll just nip up there myself and see him.'

I walk across the park to the eastern lodge, where Simpkin has lived all of my life. There is an old hunting gate, hanging off its hinges, that separates the lodge from the park. Beyond it, ironically, is a rough old patch of garden, just long grass dotted with penny moons, butter-cups and freckle-throated foxgloves. The crumbling brick path leads to the front door, which is newly painted – like all the other cottage doors and window frames on the estate – in Harlington Green gloss. The door opens straight into the living room, where Simpkin sits, slumped in a woven rattan bathchair, a yellow and green tartan rug pulled over his knees. His face is waxy white and his eyes, lips and even his hair seem colourless, as though they have all been carved out of a single piece of soapstone. I can hear his breathing, rattlesnake breaths, reverberating, as I stand, suddenly gasping for air myself, in the doorway.

I should take him right now, I think, return him to the hospital, but he seems to read my mind.

'Sir,' he says, 'I want to be here.' His voice sounds strangled as though he is trying to make himself heard through thick treacle. 'I will be better if I can see the roses. They will flower soon.'

'Yes, of course,' I say. 'I do understand.' I take the tape from my pocket.

'Do you have a cassette player? I have something for you here.'

I find the player next to the old, scratched gramo-phone on the side table. There are shelves above of 78s, corrugated lines of brown cardboard spines and three tiers of dowelling cassette racks packed with Simpkin's music collection. I put the tape in the machine. 'It's the Galos, isn't it?' he says. His colourless eyes reflect the sun that is setting over the park. He pushes his hands down on the wheels of the chair and moves himself to the door, gazes across the gardens, towards the roses. I press Play on the machine and the first bass notes sound in the tiny room.

The music hasn't got far, before, with a bum note, it stops, abruptly. I hear my own voice on the tape, exclaiming: 'Oh bugger!' I look at Simpkin. My expletive has made him laugh, a viscous, bubbling cough, and he is clutching at his chest. And then the music starts again. I stand next to Simpkin as he looks far away, further than the roses, much further than the gardens or the park. He speaks in barely a whisper as the speakers deliver my grand piano to his low-beamed, stifling room.

'There,' he whispers, 'the wind is getting up. There are ripples on the lake . . . they are getting bigger now, each ripple running into the next . . . they are almost like waves.' He is smiling, his eyes shut now. His head and shoulders sway above the tartan rug as the piano builds in a crescendo. His large hands move, free of inhibition as the music gets softer again: 'And now the wind is dropping and the trees are quiet again . . . the lake is still, like glass. There is peace now.' The piano is silent, the last chord echoing for just a moment, before it is replaced by my own voice filling Simpkin's room from the speakers: 'There, I've done it. Fiona can stop pestering me now and the old fool can pop his clogs and have this at his funeral. To Simpkin.' And then there is the sound of laughter and glasses clinking, as my own voice is joined by others, slurring, 'To Simpkin!'

I knock a lamp to the floor, my own laughter ringing remorselessly in my ears, where it shatters into smithereens as I leap across Simpkin's room, fumbling for the Stop button. I turn around, my shameface burning, to see that Simpkin has got up from his chair and is stumbling across the gardens. I watch, as a sudden pain like a knife twisting inside my chest makes my eyes water, I watch Simpkin as he walks through the fading light towards the orangery and the moss roses that I can see silhouetted before him.

The Right Girl
for the Job

The metallic-blue hatchback stopped on the double yellow lines outside the church hall and the woman driver swivelled in her seat, stretched to open the back door and, still sitting at the wheel, ushered the two small children out into the rain. The girl, mature for her four years in black patent buckled shoes and with wispy fair plaits sticking out at ninety degrees from her head, took her younger brother's hand and led him down the steps and through the crypt door to join the other children at their Montessori nursery school. The woman did not get out but watched them through the car window, engine still running.

She hadn't always been like this. When the girl first started at the school, her mother always took her into the hall, helped her to hang her coat on the peg marked with her name sticker and exchanged pleasantries with Miss

Rosaleen, the nursery teacher, before leaving with her little brother hugged into her, his chubby legs gripped to either side of her hip like a nutcracker. Sometimes she would stay at home with the baby boy and the girl's father took their daughter into the school, swinging her in his arms as he made his way down the brickwork steps, noses rubbed like Eskimos before he made his dash back to the car, defeating the quickstep of the traffic warden, and from there to his desk at the ad agency.

But these days their mother felt too dishevelled to show her early-morning face to the world or even to Miss Rosaleen, what with the single parent's mad morning dash of lost shoes and spilt Rice Krispies, of the little boy's soaking pyjamas and sheets, of the packed lunches to be made for both children and the nursery's spare pants and trousers to be returned, clean and ironed, after her small son's habitual accidents. The mother's own hair went unbrushed, her throat and mouth stale from the night, her worries waiting, biding their time, as she persuaded the boy into his tracksuit and her daughter into the duffle coat that she despised and sulked about most mornings. Then the woman pulled on jeans and a large jumper over her nightdress and shuffled her stockingless feet into her shoes, any shoes that happened to be handy.

Letting herself back into the house, the woman would catch sight of herself in the full-length hall mirror; all hair like a witch and yesterday's make-up smearing her eyes, which reflected back at her, dull as stones. 'Well, there we have it, Caroline,' she would mutter to her reflection. 'Who, in their right mind, would want to stay with someone like you?' and she would slam down her bag on the bottom of the stairs before standing the espresso pot on the gas hob and restarting her morning. Inevitably there were wet beds to be changed and toys to be mended and promises to be kept of home-time surprises and chocolate cake. Bloody hell, she would think, what I need around here is a wife.

Alone with her black coffee in the bathroom she set about her own preparations. It took so long to get ready these days. As each year passed, the shelves by the basin looked more and more like an apothecary's, with the multiplying pots of anti-wrinkle day creams, soothing eye gels, nutrient-rich night creams, bust-firming lotions and skin tonics. Gone were the days when a dab of Nivea sufficed. Sometimes it seemed that no sooner had she anointed herself with the necessary potions than it was time to return to the school to pick up the children. At least on her return she would step out of the car and into the church hall and speak to the other parents and to Miss Rosaleen, carefully disguising the flatness of her voice, before buckling her two children back into their car seats and heading for home.

The morning of her sixth wedding anniversary, just three months since Colin had walked out, started much like any other. She had dropped the children off and was driving back up the Euston Road. A fine drizzle had started and the hanging sky was threatening heavier rain. The windscreen wipers needed replacing and screeched across the grimy windscreen, moving sooty tracks to and fro. The traffic was slow and she sat at the red lights wishing the car radio hadn't been stolen, looking at the hoardings. To the left was an advertisement for sports bras, depicting the double loops of a skipping rope. Apparently if you didn't wear one of these special garments for exercising, then your bust ended up as a sad drooping 'W', like the rope. She wondered if Colin had masterminded the ad. It was his sort of thing.

She wished the traffic lights would hurry up so that she could escape the image and get home. She had a lot to do before leaving to pick the children up again; there were eight girls coming today. The final eight in a week of interviews where not one of the applicants had been remotely suitable. 'Let one of today's be the one,' she prayed to the road ahead.

The first girl arrived early, and Caroline could see from through the bedroom window that she was just not going to get the job. She felt like shouting from where she was, 'No, no, no! You won't do at all. Go away and save us both the bother!' as she looked down on the mousy creature swaddled in tweed overcoat, sheltering under a plastic see-through umbrella. Instead, she pulled on her skirt and tights, found her brown shoes and let the girl in.

'Hallo, Mrs Belman, I'm Sarah Forrester. I'm a bit early but I got here much quicker than I expected,' she explained in a small voice, offering a pale paw with bitten nails to be shaken by the older woman.

Caroline ushered the girl into the sitting room, casting her eyes to the ceiling, and wondered how soon she could dismiss her. As Sarah Forrester talked, Caroline took in the wispy hair and sensible leather loafers and in a fug of boredom and despair learned all about her previous experience, her glowing references, her cookery and geography O levels. She managed to ask a couple of questions about the girl's upbringing and hobbies but all the time longed for Sarah Forrester to go away.

The next applicant was worse. She had obviously lied about her age on her CV and didn't look a day under thirty-five. She wore a cheap-looking suit of pale-blue viscose that was stretched tightly over her bulky hips, and on her mouth and two front teeth a lot of pink lipstick that stained the rim of her coffee cup. Caroline thought she could hear the ticking of the girl's biological clock through her slyly giggled assurances of having a 'steady fella, ever so nice he is, but definitely no plans for a wedding for a few years yet'.

Then came a girl with a bristly blonde moustache and piggy little blue eyes, and another in white stilettos with sticking plasters on her heels and a pot of vaseline that she wiped over her bare legs before going back out into the rain to the tube.

The next applicant didn't bother to turn up and Caroline sighed with relief. It was obviously going to be much harder than she'd expected to find the perfect girl for the job. It wasn't the sort of thing she could trust to an agency; besides which, it might be a little awkward to specify exactly what she was looking for. No doubt Colin would have found just the right person by now: she felt sure that in his job at the advertising agency he was plagued with girls just like the one she was looking for. After all, it was at the agency that he had employed Sky, that perfect embodiment of everything that she was not. Sky was the girl who had snatched away her husband with the lure of her sleek blonde mane, colt's legs and – as Caroline witnessed over dinner before she knew about the affair – her easy girlish laughter at his jokes. Colin obviously thought that his new love was a girl in a million but Caroline felt sure that there were plenty more out there just like her. Girls who didn't have bust-lines like skipping ropes, girls whose youthful faces shone without the aid of creams and gels, girls who didn't need to buy their beauty from the whispered assurances of the very advertisements that Colin and his team devised for products promising to bring back youth to the skin of the terminally middle-aged.

Caroline stood at the open fridge eating her lunch, scooping taramasalata from the tub with a piece of Mighty White sliced bread and dipping the previous Sunday's left-over roast potatoes into a pot of cold beef gravy. Her heart stabbed as she remembered once again that it was her wedding anniversary. They should have been having lunch in a smart restaurant right now. If it wasn't for Sky, the Chablis would be on ice, the waiter hovering, obsequious, as he waited to take their order. If it hadn't been for Sky there would have been a dozen long-stemmed roses in the tall vase on top of the piano and she would be looking forward to having sex with her husband tonight.

It was her wedding anniversary and she had almost sent Colin a card, thinking that it might annoy Sky; but common sense prevailed as she imagined him shaking his head in disbelief as he opened the envelope and his joining the sleek Sky in outrage at her 'irrational' behaviour.

Caroline had little idea of when her husband's infidelity had started but suspected that it was sooner after their son was born than Colin was letting on. Everything had seemed so perfect though: the mortgage was manageable at last, Kate, their daughter, was displaying her father's talent for words and had her mother's large brown eyes, the large brown eyes that Colin professed he could die looking into. The apple tree that they had planted in the garden to mark Kate's birth was bearing its first fruit, and the new baby boy was over the colic that had sent them both to near nervous breakdown and was settling down into a routine of proper sleeping. Caroline was beginning to lose the weight that she had put on during the last pregnancy. Sex was still a bit erratic, she had to admit, but Colin had appeared to understand that nothing suppressed a woman's desire more than breastfeeding and the hormonal challenge that it presented. Had she known then, of course, what she knew now, she would have done something about it, maybe even put the baby on to a bottle sooner.

'Oh, don't be such a silly cow,' she reprimanded herself as she finished the last potato. 'Of course the baby had to come first.' But she wasn't putting the children first now, and she knew it.

'Look, I think I should be straight with you from the outset,' said the next girl through the door. 'I'm only really interested in the job if I get sole use of a car, so do tell me now if that's not going to be possible.'

Caroline had no idea how she could afford another car, but thought, as she looked again at the girl perched on the edge of the sofa with her pretty legs set at an angle and her high heels, that maybe Colin could be persuaded to provide one. 'If you were the right girl for the job, I'm sure we could sort something out,' she said. The girl had some experience but seemed a little reluctant to talk about her last position, saying only that it had been in France and that there had been 'one or two problems with my employer's husband, if you know what I mean'.

Caroline thought she knew exactly what the girl meant as she studied her further, drinking in the berry-slicked lips, plump as satin cushions, the fluid elegance of the long white throat and the pink tongue that flicked to the corner of the marvellous mouth before she spoke in a voice as soft as caramel. 'I know I have less experience than some people of this sort of thing, but I did spend a lot of time caring for my younger brothers and sisters before my modelling work became full-time.'

'And you're no longer modelling?' asked Caroline, amazed that such a girl should be sitting opposite her now, applying for the job at all.

'No, I've had enough of dressing up for a living,' she said. 'It's time to do something more rewarding. You know, modelling really isn't everything it's cracked up to be.'

This was the one and no doubt about it, thought Caroline. She was perfect, like the 'after' pictures from a plastic surgeon's brochure. The girl's every expression, the pout, the tilt of the head and the flirtatious eyes were inescapably sexually charged. Her face was a smooth oval framed with softly curling chestnut hair that fell to below her shoulders. The eyes were slanted, green like a cat's, the lashes thick beneath arched brows.

'Well, Sophia,' said Caroline, smiling warmly, 'I think I would like to offer you the job. Of course, it's up to my husband too – not that he lives here any more, as I think I explained on the telephone, but you would have to travel with him and the children so I promised him that he could meet the prospective nanny – but I'm sure he'll agree that you are just the right girl for the job.' Sophia beamed at this news and agreed to return the following afternoon to meet Colin and discuss the terms of her employment.

Caroline poured herself a glass of the Chablis that she had bought for a lone wedding anniversary drinking binge. She actually felt happy for the first time since the day she finally found out about Colin's passion for the wretched Sky. She had been plotting her revenge ever since; it was really the only thing that kept her going through the night sweats and the sleepless nights and the children's wailing for the father who had been so callously stolen from them – along with his bedtime stories – by a girl they had never met with a very silly name. Of course she wanted Colin back, but as that didn't seem to be on the cards ('Look, Caroline,' he'd said when he left, 'this has nothing to do with Sky') she was damned if the agent of her misery should get to keep him.

While it's one thing having a husband who commits adultery it is quite another to find one's children falling joyfully, duplicitously perhaps, into the arms of another woman. And that thought spurred her on too. 'It would be like rubbing salt into the wounds,' she'd explained to Colin, trying not to cry, during one of their terse telephone conversations. She had made him promise that the children wouldn't have to meet his new girlfriend, at least not too soon after the break-up.

'I suppose you're right,' he'd conceded. 'It might be a little unsettling for them at this stage but it is something you'll have to face at sometime. Sky is really terribly sweet around children.'

Colin visited the children in their home twice a week after school, but never at weekends, when he and Sky were otherwise occupied flying to Paris or Rome or simply weekending at her parents' Queen Anne manor house in Buckinghamshire.

'Daddy says we might have another little brother or sister one day,' Kate had said excitedly while Caroline was tucking her up in bed after one of his visits. 'Does that mean you have another baby in your tummy, Mummy?'

Caroline was lost for words as the tide of salt water rose in her mouth. She hugged her daughter with her face pressed into the small girl's hair, swallowed her misery and struggled, as she had been doing since Colin's departure, not to cry in front of her. Eventually she looked down into Kate's large, expectant eyes and whispered:

'Go to sleep now, poppet. Things are not easy or simple but think how lucky you are to have such a sweet baby brother already.'

And she'd kissed her on the forehead and left the room.

★

'Why do you bother?' hissed Caroline to herself as she stood before the bathroom mirror, awaiting Colin's arrival, applying light-diffusing, age-defying make-up to the lines around her eyes. 'It's not as though you can compete with a bimbo half your age,' she continued scolding as she brushed colour on to her lips with a miniaturist's precision. Colin was due in an hour and a half to make Sophia's acquaintance, to give his stamp of approval to the goods for which he would be paying, thought Caroline as she sprayed her throat and wrists with eau de toilette.

She was always like this in the stomach-churning lull before Colin was due. Of course she fantasised about the day he would find, once again, the beautiful young girl in her who had inspired him to go down on his knees three times before she agreed to marry him. How she detested herself every time he was expected for a visit to the children. How could she, she wondered, as she buffed her nails until they shone, have such a slavish devotion to a man who had proved himself so cruel, not only to her, but to the children she had borne him? But self-hatred didn't stop her from dressing in the long pistachio-coloured dress that she had worn on their honeymoon. She still wore her wedding ring, and since he left, she had added the emerald eternity ring and the South Sea pearl drop earrings that he had bought her all those years ago.

'Daddy's coming, Daddy's coming,' sang Kate as they arrived home from school. 'When is Daddy coming? *Is* Daddy coming?' she kept asking, needing her mother's constant assurance that he would indeed soon be there, as

Caroline persuaded her into a pretty smock with a pink embroidered bodice.

'Daddy might bring new toy?' added three-year-old Tom hopefully, posing his desire as a question.

'Daddy's coming. When is Daddy coming home?' demanded Kate, deliberately ambiguous. Caroline started arranging white lilies and purple delphiniums in the green glass vase that had been Colin's mother's favourite when she was still alive.

'Daddy!' screamed Kate and Tom in unison when they saw him outlined in the frosted glass of the front door. Caroline opened the door to find herself saying hello to a void as Colin stooped at four-year-old level, his arms out-stretched. No words had been spoken, as Kate hurled herself at him, rubbing her nose against his and squealing. Tom clung to Caroline's leg, repeating, 'Daddy, Daddy, Daddy, Daddy,' in his hoarse little boy's voice, like a mantra. As she led the way to the kitchen, Caroline noticed with annoyance that Tom had managed to smear his peanut butter sandwich down the front of the pistachio-coloured dress.

As she dabbed a dishcloth at the peanut butter stains, Caroline observed, with further irritation, that Colin was wearing a new Italian linen suit and day-old stubble that rather suited his strong jaw-line. Already, he had stopped looking like her husband and more like the sort of man he might cast as the driver of some flash coupé in one of his television commercials. Or like the brooding hero of a shirt advertisement in a fashion magazine who should have some Oriental beauty draped over his shoulder. Caroline almost wondered if it were quite natural for the children to be sitting, as they were, one on each of this suave stranger's knees. The male model was handing her a packet of green tea leaves now.

'I've given up tea and coffee but this stuff is very refreshing,' he told her. 'Do have a cup, it does wonders for cleansing the system.'

'Yes, and so does castor oil,' thought Caroline, as she obediently set the kettle to boil.

Sophia arrived five minutes later. Wearing a short, smooth silvery-beige cashmere dress with a wide chocolate-coloured suede belt pulling in her tiny waist, and matching thigh-length soft suede boots, she slunk into the kitchen like a Siamese cat. Colin stood and smiled with a new shyness as she shook his hand, and then she knelt down to greet the children.

'So this is Kate,' she said to the wide-eyed little girl, and then, taking the small boy's hands in hers, 'And you must be Tom. I've heard so much about both of you from your mum.'

Colin knelt down too. 'Say hello to Sophia,' he urged his two children.

'Is green tea all right for you, Sophia, or would you prefer a coffee?' asked Caroline, as Tom clung to her legs, using her as a shield from which to peep out at the exotic stranger.

'I adore green tea,' replied the girl, sitting herself at the kitchen table and flashing her wide-mouthed smile at Caroline, who was busying herself with the teapot and measuring out the new tea leaves.

'Why don't you take Sophia to see your bedrooms while the tea is brewing?' suggested Caroline brightly to the children. Kate needed no further prompting. She took Sophia by the hand, attempting to drag her from the room. Tom stayed where he was, red in the face and rooted to the spot.

'Go on, Tom,' urged Caroline. 'Show Sophia your Thomas train set.'

'Can't,' said Tom miserably. 'Wet pants.'

'Oh Tommy, not again,' sighed his mother.

'Don't worry, Tom,' said Sophia. 'Come and show me where your clothes are kept and we'll get you changed. I bet you've got some nice Thomas the Tank Engine pyja-mas you could put on.'

'Yes, yes I have' said Tom, round-eyed, as he shuffled from the room with his sister and Sophia.

'Now, Colin, I have interviewed God knows how many girls for this job and this one is by far the best.'

'Yes,' said Colin, loosening his tie, 'she seems very nice, but are you sure she really wants to be a nanny?'

'Yes, yes, I've grilled her about that, I'm not a com-plete idiot, you know,' Caroline assured him irritably. 'She adores children, but don't worry, she doesn't want any of her own yet. She just wants a live-in post in a nice family to support her while she does an Open University English degree. If it all works out we would have her here for at least three years, which would give the children some sta-bility – what with your not being here any more.'

Colin tried a shrug, but his eyes gave him away.

'If the children like her,' he said carefully, 'and Kate certainly seems to be rather taken already, then it's fine with me. Have you discussed her salary, or is that what I'm here for?'

'Well, you did agree to pay for a nanny, so I suppose I should leave that to you,' agreed Caroline. 'Only there's one thing you should know: every single one of the nannies I interviewed expected their own car and I'm pretty sure Sophia will be the same. I know for a fact that she had one in her last job.'

Colin looked startled, and she continued, 'It's a bit shocking, I agree, but it seems to be par for the course these days.'

'Can't she just share yours?' Colin was wearing his reasonable-man-talking-to-an-imbecile look. The same patient look that Caroline had grown so used to since her first pregnancy that she had stopped even noticing it. But she noticed it now and it irritated her.

'Oh yes, sure. That would rather defeat the object, wouldn't it? I thought the whole idea of getting a nanny was to free me to take up my career again. How am I supposed to do that if the nanny has got the car?' she snapped. 'Why do you have to be so deliberately dense?'

Sophia and the children returned to the kitchen.

'Well, I must get in touch with my mother and see if she still has all my Barbie dolls,' Sophia giggled as she sat with Kate on her knee, the little girl stroking the soft arm of the Siamese cat dress. 'I can see that there's someone here who might enjoy playing with them.'

Kate glowed, blissful. Caroline poured the green tea. It tasted bitter to her but Colin and Sophia sipped with pleasure as they discussed the modelling work that Sophia had done and found that he knew one or two of the photographers she had worked with.

Colin looked at his watch.

'Damn,' he said, 'I have to meet someone at the cinema in the King's Road in ten minutes.' Caroline noted that he didn't name the someone, but she knew it was Sky. 'If it's all right with you, I'll drop by and see the children after work on Tuesday.'

As he spoke, he was looking past Caroline, through the french windows, at Sophia, who was on the lawn picking daisies with Kate and Tom. He joined them in the garden and kissed the children goodbye. 'I'll be back on Tuesday,' he promised them, and then, through the open door, Caroline heard him say, 'I'll see you then too I hope, Sophia. I suppose you'll have started with us by then?'

He looked like the cat who had got the cream as Caroline showed him out.

'I'm sure I can sort out a car for Sophia,' he purred as she held open the front door. 'Sky is due for a new company car this year and it shouldn't be much of a problem to bring it forward and buy out the one she's driving.' And with that he turned to leave.

'See you next Tuesday then,' called Caroline to the back of his Italian linen jacket as he made his way down the path.

He telephoned later that night, waking Caroline, who was dozing in front of the television.

'Good film?' she asked.

'No, not really,' he said, his voice so low it was barely more than a whisper. 'I was just phoning to remind you that we've still got quite a lot of my mother's furniture in storage. I wasn't sure if you'd remember.'

'Yes, I know that. There's a list somewhere,' replied Caroline, puzzled, but pleased that the level of his voice was excluding Sky from whatever he was trying to tell her.

'Well, I was just thinking,' said Colin, 'that spare room is a little sparse and I wondered maybe if you would like me to arrange for that nice little carved dressing table and the walnut bed to be delivered before your new nanny starts on Monday. Just a thought, but do let me know,' he half-whispered, ever so casually.

'Stupid bastard,' said Caroline, but with a sad smile, as she replaced the receiver.

As it turned out, Sophia brought beautiful things of her own to cheer up the little room at the top of the house. A golden silk tasselled eiderdown was spread over the bed and five different types of orchids in Mexican painted pots stood on the small table and the chest of drawers. Many new pictures hung on the walls, including a large watercolour of Sophia lying in a Provençal field of lavender, which she said had been painted by her father. She was true to her word and had unearthed her old dolls and an astonishing array of Barbie clothes, which she heaped in a fragrant Chinese cedar chest for Kate to play with.

The children were up in Sophia's room now, helping her to finish her unpacking, as Caroline luxuriated in a deep, steaming bath sprinkled with the ylang-ylang and camomile oils that Sophia had brought her as a present.

'I think you deserve a delicious treat. Try five drops of each, go on, right now,' she urged, handing over the little blue glass bottles.

The next day, Caroline had her first lie-in for some time while Sophia dressed and breakfasted the children and took them to school. She basked in bed, enjoying the luxury of drifting through dreams and reality, one moment finding herself supine in a field of French lavender, then sitting behind Sky on a bus with a pair of scissors, snip-snipping at the back of her hair; the next surfacing to see that it was five past ten and if she didn't get up soon, she would miss her appointment at the hairdresser. Caroline had not had her hair done since Colin had left. Sophia suggested that she ask for a henna treatment.

'Trust me,' she said. 'You would look beautiful if the red highlights in your hair were brought out.'

And that was precisely what Caroline requested when she made the appointment at Olivier Michel's, the small west London salon that Sophia recommended.

'I'm going to do a bit of shopping after I've had my hair done. Don't forget that Colin's coming over later to see the children, but I should be back by then,' said Caroline as she left Sophia, who was tidying out the pots of dried-up poster colours and stiffened glue brushes from the children's art cupboard.

'Make sure you buy something lovely to go with the new hair,' said Sophia. 'Brown's have got some fantastic new Jasper Conran stuff. You must try them on because they don't look like anything on the hanger.'

Caroline, who always found that things looked rather better on the hanger than on herself, decided that she would do just that.

In the changing cubicle at Brown's, Caroline struggled out of her clothes, despising the sight of her bra straps digging into the unwanted flesh that had accumulated on her back, and her bottom, immense to her critical eyes, netted by large greying Marks and Spencer's knickers and her control-top tights. She slipped on a dark-green Jasper Conran velvet tunic over a matching short skirt and stepped shyly from the changing room to the larger mirror outside.

'You look fabulous in that,' sighed another shopper, a woman ten years her junior, slim in jeans and a black T-shirt. 'Where did you find it? I must try it on myself.'

Caroline had to admit that she liked what she saw as she swivelled before the store's mirror. Her new hair was glinting, the hennaed highlights soft with the new cut around her face. The dark-green velvet suited her pale skin and the cut of the skirt brought focus to her legs, which had always been her best feature.

'I'll keep it on if you could just remove the security tags for me,' Caroline instructed the shop assistant, handing over the clothes she had been wearing like so many rags to be bundled up.

Outside the house when Caroline returned home was

a bright-red convertible Golf GTi that she hadn't noticed parked in the small suburban street before. It was a street of family Volvos and company BMWs and the red car looked strangely out of place.

'Hi,' said Sophia as Caroline dashed into the house, even shyer now about her new clothes and hair. 'You've just missed Colin. He brought over the car. I must say, it's a bit of a beauty. Did you notice it outside?'

Caroline said that she was glad that he had got it sorted out so promptly. Colin had even given Sophia some money to buy extra children's car seats for the new car and was returning later to see Kate and Tom.

'How thoughtful,' said Caroline.

'Mummy, you look like someone on the telly,' exclaimed Kate when Sophia brought the children home from school.

'Doesn't she look beautiful, Tom?' prompted Sophia as she hung up the children's coats, smiling with pleasure at her new employer.

'Sophia's red car goes really fast. Brmmm Brmmmm,' said Tom.

When Colin arrived he brought a pot of new French anti-wrinkle face cream for which his company had just won the account.

'Here we are, Caroline. I thought you might like this,' he said, handing it to her as though it were a holy sacrament. Caroline noticed that Sophia looked horrified, and Colin turned to her and said, 'I would have brought you one too, but I don't think you need it yet.'

'Actually, I don't think Caroline needs you to bring it for her either,' she retorted. 'She's got beautiful skin.'

Colin laughed nervously. 'Yes, yes, quite. Hum. Just wanted a bit of market feedback. No offence intended. Now where are those little devils hiding?'

The children were in Sophia's room, dressing up: Tom as a pirate in one of Sophia's long stripy T-shirts and Kate as a princess in one of her satin camisoles. When Sophia went upstairs to fetch them, Colin handed over a bottle of Sancerre and asked Caroline if it would be all right if he stayed for supper.

'I haven't had a chance to put the little ones to bed for quite a while, have I?' he explained, nervous as a teenager on his first date.

Sophia and Caroline cooked together, chopping courgettes, onions and tomatoes for ratatouille to go with the braised chicken breasts that were turning golden in the oven. Colin sniffed appreciatively as he came down from reading to the children, opened the bottle of chilled Sancerre and poured out three glasses.

'Here's to the children and their new nanny, and happy times ahead,' he toasted, raising his glass and clinking it against first Caroline's and then Sophia's. He sat between the two women, eating chicken breast, like a King in his castle, so at home it was as though he had never left.

'I've been thinking, Caroline,' he said, between mouthfuls, 'as it's your birthday next Saturday, why don't you let me take the children off your hands for the week-end?'

Caroline could have written the script for him before he even spoke. How she hated him for that.

'I don't know,' she faltered, sipping her wine, looking like a woman who might be sipping a few more glassfuls before the night was through.

'Oh, don't worry,' he said, refilling her glass. 'I can keep a promise, you know. Sky won't be there: she has to go to her parents' for the weekend for some aged uncle's birthday.'

'I suppose the children might quite like to see where you live,' said Caroline, staring hard at the brimming glass before her. 'But I think Sophia should go with them. It's important for them to have continuity of care and I would feel happier about their being away if she stayed with them.'

There, she had said it. She felt sad. She felt wicked. This was what she had been planning and her plot was working perfectly. The part of her that still loved Colin felt like calling a halt now, but the part that hated him – and more especially the part that hated Sky – was stronger. The cold spite in her head was ruling the warm pains of nostalgia in her heart as, over the remains of the bottle, she finalised the details.

Later, in bed, Caroline wept as she imagined the denouement of her carefully hatched plot: Colin with his hands in Sophia's chestnut curls, undressing her slowly, marvelling at her luscious body, whispering into her ear. She could hear Sophia's breathing, and Colin's moaning, gasping for breath as they fell on the bed, Sophia's long legs around his neck, his hands on her breasts . . .

'Stop! Stop!' she cried out loud. But stop she – and thus they – could not, and the heat of Colin and Sophia's passion stayed with her throughout the long, sleepless night.

Several times over the next few days she thought of breaking the arrangement, but then she would think about Sky, about Colin telling Kate that one day they might have another little brother or sister, about how Sky had eaten dinner at her table on two occasions without Caroline even suspecting that her foot was probably resting in Colin's crotch the entire time she was sitting there, the perfect corporate wife, believing her marriage to be sacred. She'd even told Colin how pretty and intelligent she found his new assistant to be.

By the time it came to Saturday morning she was both resolute and resigned. Sophia brought her tea in bed. The children came in and sang 'Happy Birthday'. She hugged them and thanked them for their pictures, which Sophia had framed as a surprise. Then Sophia handed her a package wrapped in white paper across which golden cherubs played lutes and tied with an extravagant gold bow.

'I'll just get the children into their coats but I want you to open this and try it on before we go,' she said, looking at Caroline with her slanting cat's eyes.

Caroline untied the bow and under the paper found a smooth, thick cardboard box. Inside that, wrapped in pink tissue paper, was the most beautiful lace slip she had ever seen. It was oyster silk with delicate shell-pink scalloped lace trim and unlike anything she had ever worn in her life.

'Go on, put it on, it's your size,' urged Sophia, reappearing at the bedroom door.

'Give me a minute then,' giggled Caroline. She went into the bathroom and carefully let the slip slither over her arms and head. The lace curved delicately around her breasts and she felt like a film star.

Sophia was at the door as Caroline stood before the mirror, the same mirror into which she had mouthed so much of her despair.

'You look like a dream,' said Sophia.

'Well, it is lovely,' said Caroline, straightening her hair, trying to pull the slip down to cover herself.

'You're beautiful,' said Sophia, 'more beautiful than you know.'

'Well . . .'

'Do you mind me saying this?'

'What?'

'You know, that you're beautiful.'

In the mirror Caroline could see Sophia approaching her, and watched fascinated as the girl's exquisite hands reached around her, embracing her while she stroked the fabric over her breasts and waist and down over her thighs.

'You're *my* dream,' she said. 'I've wanted you from the first moment I set eyes on you. Did you know that?'

Downstairs, Caroline could hear the children calling for Sophia, impatient to get to their father's new house.

'You don't need to worry about the children,' purred Sophia. 'I'll take good care of them while we're away.'

Looking for Signs

For Ben, some boxing gloves. They stood around me then, my father, my brother, my aunt and her twins. All five of them gawping at me as though I was some sort of mutant in an aquarium, waiting for me to open my present. One of the twins was jiggling on the spot. I felt like telling her to go to the bog before she wet herself, doing the pee-pee dance like that. At her age. And Aunt Vanessa had two little red spots, one on either cheek, a rash of excitement that came up just because Ben kissed her. Well, he would, wouldn't he? After she bribed him with those horrible gloves. He probably thought he could get other things out of her while she was here. I stood in the middle of their circle, weighing the square parcel in my hands, warming my cold heart against the heat of their impatience, chewing skin from my bottom lip.

'Well,' said Aunt Vanessa, after a while, 'aren't you going to open your present?'

I wanted the present, I just didn't want them there, watching me. I didn't want them there. Not at all.

'I think you'll like it,' she coaxed, 'the twins chose it specially for you.'

Oh bloody goody gum drops, I thought, and I shook the parcel while they watched and waited. Silly twins, blushing Aunt Vanessa, Ben with his terrifying puffed-up leather gloves, and my father. Then, slowly, I peeled the Sellotape from the folded flap at one end of the pink wrapping paper and slid my finger carefully along the edge.

'Pearl always likes to save the paper,' my dad explained.

I undid the other end of the parcel. Inside was a white cardboard box which I placed on the carpet at my feet. Whatever was inside could wait while I smoothed and folded the pink paper. How impatient they all were.

'Come on, Pearl, open your present.' Bossy twin.

'Have a look at what's in the box.' Other bossy twin.

'I bet it's something good.' Greedy Ben.

I knelt next to the box and slowly lifted the lid on my surprise present. And then I screamed, my loudest scream ever, and leapt straight into my father's arms.

'Take it away!' I cried. 'Get it out of here, please take it away. Take it away. *Take it away!*'

My father carried me, yelling, hysterical, up to the box room over the porch that was to be my room while Aunt Vanessa was staying to help look after Ben and me because our mother was in hospital. The twins were to sleep together in the big lace-canopied bed in my room with the lovely walls that my mother had painted herself with mermaids and dolphins and fishes all around.

'I want Moppy,' I sobbed as he stumbled into the tiny room with me rigid in his arms. 'Moppy' is what we call my mother. Her real name, Isobel, has barely been used since the day I was born. She is like me, translucently white-skinned, with the same hair of coral, each strand as thick as a horse's tail hair. You could play a violin with our hair, that's what my dad always says. And he says we smell the same way.

They named me Isobella when I was born, so like my mother was I. But then, when she was left alone with me, she looked at the milk lustre of my nude baby skin against her breast and she called me her little pearl. And it stuck after that. Apparently, my father started calling her Mop, meaning mother-of-Pearl, and that stuck too. I have always liked the way that Moppy is defined by being my mother. She told me once that it was like her life started too, that moment I was born.

There was barely room to move in the box room, what with the clutter of books and games and toys that I had piled in when Dad broke the news that I was to be ousted from my bedroom. The little bed was swamped by my double duvet, my satin cushions and a menagerie of soft toys. I didn't want those twins touching any of my stuff.

'I hate them. They just want to frighten me. Tell

them all to go away.' I screamed and screamed as my father cleared a space for me on the bed.

'Calm down, Pearl. They didn't know,' he said, still cradling my head in his arms. 'I'll go back downstairs and get rid of it right now, if you'll just stop upsetting everyone by screaming like that. I'll get you some milk and chocolate biscuits if you'll be a good girl and stop shouting.' He had to shout the last bit himself because I was making such a noise with my crying.

I pulled the duvet over my head and buried my face in my pillow, muttering still about the twins and nasty Aunt Vanessa. Under my pillow was my mother's sapphire-blue nightdress, which I wrapped around my face, and soon my hot breath released her familiar essence from the silky folds. Camomile and cloves.

When, a few minutes later, I heard footsteps coming up the stairs, I had fairly well recovered from my shock and was ready for the milk and chocolate biscuits, but instead of my dad it was Aunt Vanessa who came into the room, bringing Ben with her.

'Go away,' I said, pulling the quilt back over my head and pushing the silk nightdress down to my feet. 'I don't want you.'

'Dear Pearl, you're going to have to get used to me being here. It might be some time before your mother's well enough to look after you this time.' Her voice was steady, but she was holding Ben by the shoulders, like a hostage, in front of her.

I pulled the quilt down enough to be able to watch

them with my right eye. Ben hovered awkwardly before her in the tiny space between the bed and the window, dangling the boxing gloves, which were tied together by their laces like a pair of dead puffer fish.

'Now, come out from under your quilt,' she said. 'I think Ben has some explaining to do, haven't you, Ben?'

Ben was smirking but saying nothing as I struggled to keep the quilt over my face while Aunt Vanessa yanked at it. 'Come on, Pearl, we're going to talk about this,' she said.

'Now, the girls and I bring you a special present and all you do is scream and shout abuse at us. It's all right, I'm not cross. Ben has confessed all,' she said, folding the quilt down from my face. 'Now, my dear little girl, I can assure you that lovely dolly is *not* a shrunken dead person wrapped in plastic, isn't that right, Ben?'

Ben just looked into my face and started to puff his cheeks up with suppressed giggles, until his eyes popped and he looked as though his face would burst.

'And,' she continued, 'the psychiatric hospitals are not full of people waiting to be shrunk and turned into dolls, so you've no need to worry about your mum. Is that clear?'

Ben was still smirking and I just wanted to kill him. Who should I believe? Suppose Aunt Vanessa was tricking me? It wasn't only Ben; I had heard my dad on the telephone before, saying that my mum needed a shrink. The only thing I was sure of was that I did not want a little dead, shrunken, plastic-coated baby to play with. Not one little bit I didn't.

'Well, Ben? Pearl?' said Aunt Vanessa, plonking her bottom on the bed without asking if she could and patting me on the hand. 'Ben?'

'It was just a joke,' muttered Ben. 'She *always* believes stupid things. It's not my fault.'

'But,' said Aunt Vanessa, 'I think it *is* your fault. Terrifying poor Pearl like that. Now that wasn't very kind, was it?'

'Anyway, dolls are stupid,' he said.

Aunt Vanessa held my hand above the quilt and I stared at her puffy little fingers, like sausages, I thought, so ugly, not like Moppy's lovely lean pianist's hands at all.

'The twins have lots of dolls and doll's clothes that you can play with while we're here, Pearl. You must get over your little phobia, and your daddy agrees that we can't be hiding everything just because you walk into the room. Now, pet, that wouldn't be fair on my girls, would it? So I'm going to bring your own doll in here and we'll play with it together for a while now that you know that naughty Ben was just pulling your leg.'

I had never seen a doll really close up before and my curiosity got the better of me. With just a token expression of terror, I agreed that the doll could come into my room on the condition that my aunt would take it away the minute I asked her to. Aunt Vanessa brought the doll and showed me how it could be undressed. She removed its button-up knitted bonnet and white lacy matinée jacket and then its white cotton underclothes. She was careful to point out the obviously non-human swivelling joins of the

68

legs and arms to the shiny plastic body. The doll was all-over pink, even its baby hair moulded from the same piece of plastic as its head. When Aunt Vanessa laid it down on my bed its blue glass eyes shut behind painted tin lids, a double dead man's wink, without eyelashes. It was quite the most hideous thing I had ever seen.

With Aunt Vanessa's coaxing, I was persuaded to touch the doll and then to get it dressed again. 'I'll knit you some new outfits if you tell me what colour wool you'd like,' she promised, as I gingerly buttoned up the white jacket and bonnet. The way she went on, calling me 'pet' and all that, anyone would think she liked me.

'What will you call your dolly?' she asked, finally triumphant.

I looked at the doll in her hands, and there were those eyes. Familiar blue glassy eyes, expressionless. The unseeing eyes of a dead fish, eyes just like my mother's in the moments before she had one of her fits. That underwater stare that no one but me ever recognised. 'Moppy,' I wanted to say, 'baby Moppy,' but I knew that that would give the game away, so I said the first name that came into my head: 'Mrs Jelly.'

'Well,' said Aunt Vanessa, 'that's a strange name for a baby doll.' And she left me in the bed, cradling Mrs Jelly in my arms.

As soon as she had gone, I poked my fingers into the plastic eye sockets of the baby doll and forced the glass eyes around until the unblinking flesh-painted tin lids were all that looked out from Mrs Jelly's face.

I always knew just by looking into her eyes when Moppy was going to behave badly. I would come down to breakfast and find her already sitting at the table, so quiet, staring from behind the blue glass of her eyes and always wearing the sapphire silk nightdress with the batwing sleeves. If we stayed in the house, she would sit there all day, which could be quite frightening, as she didn't hear a word that my dad or Ben said to her. She wouldn't hear the telephone or the doorbell, she neither cooked nor ate and we would all move around her, unobtrusive as shadows, trying to behave as though nothing were amiss. I hated to leave her sitting there like that, and so, as soon as I recognised the look in her eyes, I would feign a stomach upset or a headache and refuse to leave for school.

My dad must have known that things were going quite badly wrong. Whenever he left us there, he took these big, reluctant, tiptoey steps, like one of the Woodentops, and wrote down his number at work in thick black felt-tip as though I was too stupid to read it out of the phone book. Ben, on the other hand, always seemed relieved to get out of the house and Moppy's strangeness only seriously troubled him the once, when he asked for boxing gloves for his birthday. Sadly, our dad had to explain to him that this was quite out of the question as Moppy had developed a mortal fear of gloves of all kinds. Ben got one of his nosebleeds then, and Moppy just sat uselessly at the kitchen table and stared through him, instead of holding his head back with one of the ice-packs that she kept in the fridge.

When they left for the day, Moppy and I would go out on what she called 'a mission'. As the months passed and her illness escalated, these missions became more and more bizarre. It all started innocently enough.

'Come on, Pearl,' she said, helping me into my duffel coat from the sleeves of which two strings were hanging where, until Moppy's scissors snipped twice, there used to be mittens, 'we have work to do today.'

From the speechless torpor of the morning, she would become quite vibrant in her madness, coral hair sticking right up from her face, the dead fish eyes suddenly lit like stars. Often the mission involved standing at the iron gates of the local park from eleven o'clock until lunchtime and counting the number of redheads and fellow ginger-nuts who passed through. If there were more than thirteen in the two hours allotted to the task, then everything was fine and, she said, we would not be harmed. Then she would be light again, and we would link arms and skip into the park ourselves and eat what she called iced rats, those delicious yeasty buns with thick white fondant topping, and drink teas with as many sugars as I cared to stir into the styrofoam cup. Then I could play on the swings and the big slide while Moppy sat under the spreading branches of sweet chestnut, drafting letters to newspapers in green biro in one of her red leather notebooks.

Luckily, there were usually plenty of red- and ginger-haired people who used the park but there was a tense moment on one of the visits when we had only counted in eleven people by the time Moppy's watch said ten to one. She kept asking people the time, and shaking her watch, and she had tears rolling down her cheeks. 'They will harm us, Pearl,' she kept saying. 'We have ten minutes before they will attack.' I didn't have the faintest idea who 'they' were, nor what they would do to us, but I was as desperate as she was as the minutes ticked by and only two Japanese boys and a woman with a grey bun passed us at the gates. Our salvation arrived at three minutes to one, in the form of a flame-haired mother pushing a pram, with – yes! – a matching orange-topped baby boy inside. For one ghastly moment, I thought they were going to walk right on by but the woman hesitated for an agonising second at the gates and then turned the pram and went through into the park. Moppy and I let out a duet of relieved sighs and followed them in.

Most of Moppy's missions involved looking for signs of one sort or another. Sometimes it would take us over an hour to get to the park in the first place, although it was only a ten-minute walk. This was because of hazards on the way, like ambulances, men with umbrellas, or litter. If an ambulance passed us, we held our collars until we saw a cat; a man with an umbrella meant that we had to retrace our footsteps *backwards* until we arrived back at our front door, from where we could start again on our way; and all litter had to be picked up and posted through the letterbox of the first house on the opposite side of the street with a black front door.

'We have to do our bit if we are to survive,' Moppy

explained. It was such fun, like an elaborate game of for-feits or knock-down-ginger, but all very serious to my mother.

The bad things were gloves, especially men with gloves, and it was gloves that proved her downfall. On the day that she was taken away, we were taking the bus to the dentist, leaving plenty of time before my appointment for any missions on the way. Unfortunately, when the con-ductor came to collect our fares, Moppy noticed what he was wearing on his hands: oh, they were so snug-fitting, those gloves, with wrinkles at each knuckle, stretchy navy blue. The sort of gloves that a strangler might choose. She started screaming as though he were killing her, which was what she was trying to warn the other passengers he had in mind. The conductor pulled the emergency bell as Moppy, shielding her eyes with one arm, started swiping at him with her bag. I had to pull her off the bus before it properly stopped and she fell in the gutter with me on top of her and the conductor still shouting and waving a navy-blue fist at her from the back of the bus.

By this time, Moppy had turned her attention to car number plates, and all our missions now were further complicated by the messages that she read in them. Once, on the way to the park, a red car stopped at the traffic lights with a number plate that began PLO, and Moppy stopped me right there in the street, fumbling in her bag and then, on finding her vanity case, smearing both her own and my lips with blood-red lipstick. 'See,' she said, pointing to the accelerating car, 'that's an important car, you have to obey the red ones, and it says PLO – Put Lipstick On.' I felt foolish then, as we marched along the streets with people staring at us with our clumsy red mouths.

People with gloves, men with umbrellas and all sorts of number plates on red cars (for example, 'HTC', a common local prefix, meant 'Here They Come') could send her running and screaming home, where she hid beneath the bedcovers, trembling in the blue nightdress, which, she said, was her only protection from 'them'.

Now, as we lay on the pavement, with Moppy still shrieking, I looked at the back of the departing bus. Its number plate was MAD 631D. I was so glad that Moppy hadn't noticed it as we got up and brushed the dust from our coats.

Luckily, it was a fine day and we didn't see any men with umbrellas as we walked the rest of the way, so we were not late for my appointment. I had a raging toothache, probably from all the syrupy tea and buns I had been consuming in the park, and I hadn't been to the dentist for over a year.

We took the three flights of stairs up to Mr Collins' surgery because Moppy was frightened of the lift, and arrived panting at the receptionist's desk.

'Take a seat in the waiting room,' said the pretty Scottish girl behind the desk, once she had finished her phone call.

'No,' I said. 'My mum and I want to wait here, thanks.' I had already noticed a child through the glass door of the waiting room who appeared to be wearing woolly gloves, rainbow-striped ones, and my tooth was aching too much to risk another scene.

'As you like,' said the girl, looking at me as though I was some sort of idiot. 'You're next in in any case.'

She returned to her big black bookings diary and ignored us as we stood by the desk, even though Moppy was still visibly shaking from her encounter on the bus.

'We were lucky to escape that time, Pearl,' she was muttering. 'That was really a very close thing, we were lucky to escape that time,' and I just squeezed her trembling fingers and told her not to worry.

She'd calmed down a bit by the time the bell rang on the reception desk and the girl told us that Mr Collins was ready for me.

'Do take a seat in the waiting room,' she told my mother. 'You look like you could do with taking the weight off your feet.'

For one terrible moment I thought that Moppy was going to do just that and that she would encounter the rainbow gloves, but I kept hold of her hand, refusing to go in without her.

'But Pearl,' she protested, 'there's really no need, you've always been so brave about the dentist, it's Ben who's the little coward.'

'What appears to be the problem, Pearl?' asked Mr Collins after I'd slid with relief on to his thrilling turquoise vinyl hydraulic chair and blinked up at the light. It was pointless his asking, as I had my mouth open while he poked around inside with his mirror on a stick. Dentists always do that: they ask questions or start interesting conversations while they have your mouth jammed open, or else they call you by the wrong name and you can't even correct them. And they all have smelly breath. Mr Collins' smelt of eggy bread.

'Right,' he said, removing his mirror and turning to Moppy, who was standing by his desk at the far end of the surgery, 'I think I need to fill that back molar. She's got quite a cavity there but the X-rays don't show any sign of infection so that should be all she needs today. Just the one little filling.'

And then he did it. He tidied his tray of tools, filled a metal syringe to deaden the pain of his drilling, placed it next to the drill and from a little box with a slot in the top, just like a box of tissues, pulled out a pair of powder-dusted white surgical gloves. He stretched one over his left hand with a little ping as the latex snapped over his wrist and then started wriggling his right hand into the other. 'No,' I wanted to scream as I looked over at Moppy, but I was already too late. She flew across the surgery, yelling in Polish and English: '*Ty świnio*, you bastard,' and sent his drill and his trays of tools and the syringe flying. She scratched at his face, screaming that he was not to kill us.

Mr Collins pushed her back. 'Bloody hell, woman, what do you think you're doing?' but she charged again, this time grabbing me and pulling me off the hydraulic chair and with her to a corner, where she held me before her like a shield.

'You'll have to kill the child first if you're going to do it. I don't want her to see me die.' And then, still holding me, she was shaking and sobbing, curling herself into a ball.

The Scottish receptionist came running. She must have called my father's office, and then she returned to pacify Moppy, whose hands were bleeding from beating her fists against the floor. My father came, a doctor came, and my mother was suddenly comatose, just a pile of rags, as she accepted her fate and the syringe that the doctor stuck into her arm while my dad stroked her hair and told her that everything would be all right now.

That was two weeks before I lost my mermaid's bedroom to the twins and gained Mrs Jelly and other interfering gestures from my Aunt Vanessa. Old goody-two-shoes wasted little time before she offered to come and help out her little brother, my dad. 'Look here, Pearl, it's really kind of her to drop everything while Moppy's in hospital,' he said, but I wasn't surprised that she came running over, all charitable like that. I knew that she lived in a horrible little pebbledashed house with a crazy-paved-over garden, because I had been there to stay when my mum was ill before. Those twins, they were always jealous because we had lawns at the front and the back, and a big sandpit, a fish pond and our own swing.

We didn't have to eat in the kitchen like they did at Aunt Vanessa's but had a separate dining room with a long mahogany table and ten matching chairs that had belonged to Moppy's family in Warsaw and were all that was left, she told me, of the family's riches after Hitler, or someone like that, stole everything. That was why I didn't have grandparents, she explained, because of this Hitler, and that was why people spat at her during the war. I didn't understand a thing about any of that, although I heard people saying that she had suffered. My dad told Aunt Vanessa that she had seen some terrible things in the war, and then Aunt Vanessa saw me standing there and said, 'Sshh,' and made me sit on her lap while she cuddled me and said, 'There, there, my little pet.' Well, I wasn't her little pet and I didn't like her scratchy skirt beneath my legs.

What I did know was that Aunt Vanessa was now profiting from Moppy's illness by moving in with us, and eating at her dining table. I resented seeing her there, with my cousins, the twins. I furiously watched their little blonde spaniel heads dip as they spooned tomato soup from the front of the bowl to the back and up to their mouths without slurping. Moppy once told me that Vanessa's husband had left her before the twins were even born. 'And who could blame him?' she said, with the wickedness in her eyes.

Resent them? You bet I did, but that was as ice compared to the hot spurts of hatred that followed. It was all Aunt Vanessa's fault that I was sent to bed in disgrace, because she kicked up a stink when she saw what I had done to Mrs Jelly's eyes.

'Now that's not very nice,' she said. 'Give the doll to me and I will fix it.'

'No,' I said, 'I prefer her like this.'

'What a silly girl you are, Pearl, I didn't buy you a nice doll so that you could ruin it, you know.' She was looking sorrowfully at Mrs Jelly's face.

'You gave it to me, so it's mine to do what I like with,' I said, and then added, 'Anyway, I hate the doll and I hate you.'

Unfortunately, my father heard the last bit and, with a shuddering sadness, sent me upstairs to bed. I got in, of course, without bothering to brush my teeth or get undressed, and reached under my pillow for Moppy's nightdress. But it wasn't there and I stamped back downstairs to the kitchen in time to catch one of the twins sitting on my dad's knee while Ben and the other twin licked chocolate cake mixture from the two metal beaters of the blender.

'Someone has taken something that's mine from my bed,' I said, looking through hot eyes at the cosy domestic scene before me.

Aunt Vanessa slid her cake tins into the oven before looking up and wiping her hands on Moppy's apron.

'Yes, I expect you mean your mother's blue nightie,' she said, and the twin who was still sitting on my dad's lap giggled.

'I found it there when I was making your bed and thought we should wash it and press it and take it to your mother when we visit her tomorrow. You can't have too many nighties when you're stuck in hospital, you know, and it's such a pretty one . . .'

Her voice tailed off as she saw the look on my face. I made it back to bed before the tears started.

Ben and I had not been allowed to visit Moppy at the hospital until then. She was sitting up in bed, in a little white room without a window in it. She was like our mother, but diminished, as though she had faded in the wash. The most extraordinary thing was her hair, which was no longer the same colour as mine but stuck up from her head like rusty wire wool. She looked at us blankly from mussel-shell eyes and sighed. Ben sat on one side of the bed, holding her pale hand, but I flung myself at her, burying my head in her neck and searching for the smell of camomile and cloves, but found only the bleach of the hospital.

'Ben and Pearl, I do hope you've been good children for your dad and Vanessa,' she said with a stranger's voice, distant as someone reading the news.

'Oh yes,' said Aunt Vanessa, patting her fidgeting hand. 'Isobel, you don't need to worry about a thing, they've been angels, the pair of them.' Moppy looked even sadder then, and Aunt Vanessa laid the blue nightdress on the bed.

'Look,' she said, 'I found your lovely silk nightie and it's all clean and pressed for you. You'll be the most glamorous patient they've ever seen if you wear that.'

I think Moppy saw the look on my face as I stared longingly from her to the nightdress. I think she read it well, but then she always knew what I was thinking. 'Here,' she said, pulling the laundered blue silk between her fingers, 'let Pearl look after this for me. I'll be home soon.' And she placed the nightdress in my hands and a kiss on the top of my head as I looked sideways at Aunt Vanessa's puckering lips and smiled. Soon after that, Aunt Vanessa had to take Ben and me down to the café while our dad spent some time alone with Moppy, and even Ben cried then.

Of course, Aunt Vanessa spoiled everything. The nightdress wasn't the same, it just didn't smell right, and I had trouble sleeping most nights after that. I had been up for most of the night the day before my dad announced that we were all going to Chelston Sands. 'I think we could do with some sea air, and maybe the water will even be warm enough for a swim,' he said.

'Oh, fantastic, I'm going to wear my new bikini under my dress,' said one of the twins, and the other one asked if there were any donkeys on the beach that we could ride. I looked at Ben and he at me. I knew that we were both think-ing the same thing. Chelston Sands was Moppy's favourite place in the world, and the last time we went there, we buried her up to her neck in the sand and she lay there, smil-ing and laughing and telling us that this was our special, secret place. There were certainly no donkeys at Chelston Sands; it was a wild, deserted beach that you could only reach if you walked about a mile down a rutted track and then climbed sand dune mountains where clumps of sea pinks grew. We picked the flowers and threaded them in her hair as she lay, delighted, with the setting sun turning her face to amber.

'Tell them we're not going,' I said, when Ben and I convened by the fish pond. Ben threw in some crumbs from his toast, and our two goldfish swam to the surface, parting the weeds, to gulp at the food.

'Oh, what's the point?' he said. 'There'll only be a row. Let's just go and not tell Moppy. She wouldn't really mind, anyway.'

'Yes she would,' I said, 'but they only won't go if we both refuse. Nobody ever listens to me but they always do whatever you say.'

'Honestly, Pearl, there's no point,' he said, eager for an easy life, 'and anyway, it'll be fun. I want to see if that enormous crab's still there.'

'I don't want to go with that horrible woman,' I said.

'She's not horrible, she's just trying to help us, that's all.'

'You never do anything I say,' I said, and then, 'I hate you.'

Ben shrugged his shoulders and went in to see if he could find his mask and snorkel.

Aunt Vanessa packed Moppy's picnic basket with Dairylea sandwiches, crisps, a large bottle of Tizer, some apples and two of her chocolate cakes which Ben and the twins had decorated with Smarties. The cakes looked a real mess and I wouldn't eat any if they paid me to. Then my dad let the twins swing the basket between them to the car.

'Pearl,' he said, as he helped them heave Moppy's basket into the back of our estate car, 'I'm afraid you'll have to travel in the back with this as you're the littlest.'

'But why can't one of them go in the back?' I said, pointing at the twins, who were standing one either side of him. 'It's our car, not theirs.'

'That's a very rude thing to say,' he said. 'I won't have all this constant arguing. It'll be perfectly comfortable for you in there, you'll have the blanket and all these jumpers and coats to sit on.'

'It's not fair,' I said, feeling the tears prick at my eyes, and then, 'I hate you all.'

'And you have to stop saying you hate people. Hate is a really horrid word and I won't have it.' He was very cross with me then and I decided that I wouldn't speak to any of them all day, to punish them.

'Right,' said Aunt Vanessa from Moppy's seat next to my father, as we left the town and headed up the dual carriageway, 'let's play a game. First person to spot a sign meaning "roadworks ahead" wins ten pence.'

'That's the red triangle with the man in it who looks like he's trying to put up an umbrella,' added my father.

I watched the three blonde heads bobbing in front of me as they passed a bag of Peanut Treats between them. Ben was winning the game – he had already spotted two roadworks' signs – so Aunt Vanessa changed the challenge to fifty pee for the first person to see the sea.

As we reached the top of the hill, I looked across the fields, at the patchwork of brown corduroy and green serge, and the yellow nylon squares of oilseed rape, and saw the shimmering distant band of blue before they did. But I wasn't playing, and anyway, even if I had been talking to anyone, they wouldn't have been able to hear me properly from the boot.

'The sea, the sea,' cried Ben. 'I just saw it then before

we turned the corner,' and I could see his smirk in profile as he passed the sweets over to the twins. He knew how much I liked Peanut Treats.

I had the rough wool of my dad's green oiled jumper between my fingers.

'And there's more roadworks ahead,' said Ben, as he spotted yet another man with an umbrella.

I took the jumper in my hands because I didn't want to get blood on them, and I leaned forward and put it over his face. Then I twisted his nose as hard as I could, until I could feel the cartilage crack beneath the wool. Blood spurted out from under the jumper and Ben screamed.

'Oh my God, what's going on back there?' cried Aunt Vanessa, swivelling in her seat, as my father swerved on to the hard shoulder.

Aunt Vanessa held Ben's head back and the blood spattered down her cream cardigan. Our dad opened the boot and hauled me out, into the hot diesel fumes.

'You stupid girl, what did you do that for?' he asked.

But I couldn't answer. I saw them all, the guppy-mouthed twins in the back seat, the red spurting from Ben's nose, Aunt Vanessa's blood-covered hands, and the anguished furrowing of my father's brow while he shook me. But everything was blending in with the road and the traffic and the banks of shingle rising from the hard shoulder, and his voice sounded like he was shouting underwater. I just stood there and stared and I knew that my glassy blue eyes were expressionless as a dead fish.

L y i n g   i n   B e d

Sally glared at the fat bouquet. Not one flower she liked. All pink. Candy-floss carnations, rat's-tailed chrysanthemums, sad pastel tulips on bleeding stalks and acid-yellow foliage, bound in crackly cellophane and tied with a cerise raffia bow like the sash from a spoiled child's party dress. Just for a moment, when she read the card's enigmatic 'No clues', she had allowed herself to think that they might not be from Gregory at all, but from somebody, indeed anybody, else. Just a moment's hope, all too soon dashed by his voice on the telephone.

He rang – of course – to wish her a happy Valentine's Day and, when she was silent, to enquire if she had received any nice flowers. 'No, not one,' she snapped, leaving him to fulminate against the local Interflora.

Soon after that came the engagement. To irritate her

parents she accepted his proposal – of engagement, that was, for she had little intention of marrying him. The ring sat on her third finger like a pulled molar, its one tiny diamond glinting evilly from the lump of amalgam that was the jeweller's misguided attempt to bolster the picayune stone. As it turned out, her parents protested not at all. They bought her a Staffordshire tea service decorated with orange flowers – 'For your bottom drawer,' they said – and promised her the very bed in which she had been born as a wedding gift.

Sally's parents hadn't always been so keen: Sally's early descriptions of Gregory had seen to that.

'He's rather handsome, considering he's almost as old as you, Dad,' she said, causing her mother to leave the room ('Oh dear, I think I've left something burning in the oven') and her father to feign new interest in his out-of-date copy of the *New Statesman*. Sally continued, pushing for a reaction: 'Forgetting her politics, Dad, but do you find Margaret Thatcher at all attractive?' She giggled. 'Because Gregory does. He says her eyes are full of fire.' Her father obviously wasn't in the mood to discuss the finer features of a prime minister he loathed.

Sally joined her mother in the kitchen and, sniffing appreciatively at the hot cherry loaf, asked her if she had ever met a man who actually enjoyed his schooldays: 'You see, that's what I find quite odd about Gregory. He says Harrow was the best time of his life and in those days it must have been quite tough, don't you think?'

Her mother was tight-lipped. 'I'm sure lots of people enjoy school for all sorts of reasons,' was all she said.

'Yes, but it is quite odd to reminisce fondly about the ice being broken on the swimming pool in winter before being made to swim a length before breakfast every morning. Well, I think it is anyway.' Sally found she was talking to herself, as was usual when she had these bouts of what the family termed 'severe mentionitis' of the latest man in her life. These crushes never lasted long and her parents had learnt that it was simpler not to say too much.

'If you really think you'll be happy with a Tory . . .' said her mother weakly, returning to the sitting room with a tray of buttered cherry toast and Sally trailing behind her. 'I know I wouldn't be. But you know, dear, we just want you to be happy.'

And now her happiness seemed to have taken a back seat in everyone's minds. No sooner had Gregory become her very own live-in boyfriend than they had started almost campaigning on his behalf for some sort of commitment from her.

'You've made your bed and now you must lie in it,' hissed her mother, just the once, before returning to her father and Gregory, who were discussing nationalised industries in the sitting room. Sally half-expected her to produce the wall calendar, imagining the nib of her Parker flashing as she flicked through the summer Saturdays, then asking the vicar to check the availability of the local church.

'God forbid,' she muttered to herself.

None of this endeared Gregory to her. The cherry brandy chocolates and crystallised violets that he bought her, without fail, each Thursday ('In celebration of the day we met') were, she felt sure, a plot to make her fat and ensure that no one else would fancy her. She always left them, pointedly unopened, in the fridge. Whenever she picked a fight with him (which was usually on Fridays, after she had breakfasted on cherry brandy chocolates and crystallised violets) he always sent a dozen white roses with one red one ('My bleeding heart') from Pulbrook and Gould. Her horrified colleagues watched them wilt, in central-heated agony, often sending secretaries scurrying for vases and mercy jugs of water.

Birthdays, Christmases and Valentine's Days were always especially problematic for Sally. She rather envied Rachel from the office, who was never short of inspiration when it came to her husband Lenny's birthday, or indeed any day at all that she happened to spy something in a shop window that might tickle his fancy. Sally and Rachel would wander through Covent Garden in their lunch hour, chatting about this and that, when suddenly Rachel would dive into a shop and emerge triumphant with a blue lamp, its shade embellished with a huge red and yellow Superman 'S', or with a particularly fine vintage digital watch, chunky as a child's robot with its flashing red LED display.

'Oh, Lenny will love this,' tinkled Rachel on these occasions, dragging Sally along to the local Paperchase to complete his delight with oh-so-carefully selected black tissue wrapping paper and regal purple satin bows.

Sally never saw anything in any shop that she wanted to buy for Gregory. She had endured two of his birthdays, two Christmases and now this, their second Valentine's Day. Few things depressed her more than trailing forlornly around not just Covent Garden, but Soho, Marylebone High Street, the Conran shop at Brompton Cross, Kensington High Street and even Harrods, resenting the time it was taking, looking with unseeing eyes and eventually, in desperation, spending more money than she could reasonably afford on something to salve her guilt. A CD player (but no CDs), a Mulberry pigskin briefcase, a Burberry raincoat. Gregory took each of these gifts as reassurance that she loved him very much indeed.

So why, you might ask, did Sally stay with him? It certainly wasn't the sex. Good grief, no, it wasn't that. Gregory was a kind and courteous lover, always keen to check that Sally really did want to 'make love' (never 'shag', 'screw' or 'fuck', of course). In bed – always in bed – he was careful to turn out the light, pay equal attention to each of her breasts in turn, chaste lips brushing them like a politician kissing babies, and check that she was perfectly comfortable before he cautiously penetrated her. She had managed to have an orgasm once – only once – but that had broken his concentration and thus his rhythm, and he'd looked down at her, his face a rictus of concern, and asked, 'Are you all right? Oh dear, I'm not hurting you, am I?'

Sally had groaned and turned her face to the wall. Gregory was even more gentle with her after that, and however much she tried to fantasise that he was someone else, she never again orgasmed in his company.

No, it wasn't sex that bound Sally to Gregory. It was guilt. He was her prize. They had met and secretly dined together a few times before she finally won him. When she did, it felt a bit like going home with a big stuffed toy from the fairground. They always seem so covetable swinging from the roof of that stall, while you roll ping-pong balls down a shute, or throw tatty darts at playing cards, don't they? And then you do it, you stick the darts in three royal cards or your ping-pong balls add up to twenty-one, and you leave the dazzle and noise of the fairground behind as you haul your hideous prize through the jostling crowds. Then you are home, stuck with finding a place in your life for a huge pink rabbit made out of cheap nylon fur, with a stupid expression, badly sewn seams and a rather second-hand smell.

That was how it was for Sally when she found she had Gregory all to herself. She had been drunk at a party. Gregory was drunk too. They wound up upstairs, and were undressing each other in a room full of coats (ironically, the one passionate moment of their entire relationship) when someone walked in and turned on the light. Now this would have been bad enough, but it was worse – that someone was his wife.

After his wife's subsequent miscarriage (five years of fertility treatment and the marriage over, just like that), Gregory, with Sally's advice, gave her everything. The house in Putney, the wedding silver, the Tiffany lamp and most of their mutual friends too. Gregory was brave in the face of this loss:

'At least I've got you,' he said, imprisoning Sally in his arms. 'That makes up for everything.'

'I should have left years ago,' he lied, as he arrived with his tawdry cardboard boxes and carrier bags at her flat. Sally watched as he unpacked a bag of his own toys, despising his tender gaze as he handled the tatty remnants from his childhood, watery-eyed and sentimental. A plush pink pig now adorned her bed, out of synch with the minimalist futon with its raw cotton quilt, and the deliberately bare walls. Worse still was a pale-blue musical box, painted with what Gregory called 'bunny rabbits', which now sat on the shelf with her collection of vinyl records. She wanted to scream every time he wound the wretched thing up and sang along to 'The Teddy Bears' Picnic'.

'Yes please, a nice quiet table for my fiancée and me.' Sally cringed at the word 'fiancée' as she heard Gregory's voice on the telephone booking the restaurant for their Valentine's Day dinner. He had spent the previous day in hospital, at her request. The mole on his back, that raw-chicken-coloured growth, big as a jelly tot capped with another more knobbly miniature mole and sprouting hairs at its summit, was no more. 'Benign,' said the doctor, but it had been anything but benign to Sally. She hadn't really noticed it at first, but as time went by it became so much the focus of her disgust that it festered in her mind until it was as big as a slug. Its days were numbered.

Sally felt guilty when Gregory arrived back at the flat with four stitches holding together the sliced skin where all his life the mole had been. 'It's going to leave a scar,' he said, shirt raised, forcing her to inspect the damage. Sally felt sadder than ever: she knew that she would grow to hate that scar with as much revulsion as the mole that she could see in her mind, its stalk seeping into a Petrie dish at the hospital.

So at dinner she was trying hard to be pleasant to him. Well, the truth of this was that she was trying to force herself to fancy him, what with its being Valentine's Day and the predictability of his expectation for later in bed. Gregory had a fine face, with lots of would-be-curly hair that was cut too short, and an aquiline nose. Sally cast her mind back to their night of passion in the bedroom at the party. His shirt off, the curling of hair on his chest, the sur-prise of his upper arms (more muscular than she had expected), the sight of her own legs, so brown against the lean whiteness of his thighs. She hadn't yet discovered the cheesy-coloured underarm hairs revealed in the mornings as he lay with his arms behind his head. She hadn't yet inspected the foxy brush of his pubic hair. Neither had she experienced bathing in his soupy bath after he had used up all the hot water, and the unpleasant discovery of the small, stiff orangey hair on the soap and of smelling him later on her hair.

She hadn't known about the mole then, either. She tried not to think about it now. She tried not to think about the place on his back where it had been and the puckered skin rising between the black stitches.

She sat on the velvet banquette, looking out over the

restaurant: at the table of office workers celebrating a birth-day with pink champagne and innuendo; at the married couple, silent, but mirroring each other exactly over their plates of pasta, forks rising and falling in perfect unison, chewing and sipping their Pouilly-Fumé as though they were still at home. She looked at the beautiful young man with dark hair and a charcoal jacket whose girlfriend was playing with the candle that lit the table between them. Sally thought she could see tears in the woman's eyes. Gregory talked incessantly, looked at her with the bright eyes of a child, laughed at anything she said, believing her to be a comic genius, even when she was trying to make a serious point. 'My little chickadee,' he called her. Chickenshit, she thought. While she sipped at the thick red wine, he leaned over and tenderly pushed a stray strand of her hair from her eyes and tucked it behind her ear.

Gregory was still talking as he spooned risotto into his mouth. 'So I thought to myself, that doctor looks familiar,' he said, continuing his reminiscences about his afternoon at the hospital, 'and it turns out that he's Geoff who lives over the road from the old marital home and used to come to our summer croquet party. Isn't it a small world?' 'The old marital home' was often referred to by Gregory and unleashed a terrible fear in Sally. It was the terror of the condemned, of the prisoner who is forced to come face to face with her crime. She knew all about the old marital home and what she had deprived him of. She knew about the old marital antique bidet decorated with cherubs, she knew about the old marital holidays with friends from university days and she knew how much fun those friends had at the annual old marital croquet party. She knew too that the old marital home had cherry trees lining its drive, because when she and Gregory first had their few illicit meetings, his old marital silver Alfa Romeo had been covered in pink blossom.

'Anyway, we got talking while we were waiting for the anaesthetist and he's a nice enough chap, although I seem to remember his wife is a bit dull,' continued Gregory, his chosen dish of risotto of squid simmered in black ink staining his teeth as he spoke. 'I've invited them round to dinner on Saturday. It's really the least I could do, given what a good job he did on the old back,' he added, the black ink showing up the hairline crosshatching of the forty-five-year-old enamel like the glaze on old pottery. She was paying her penance all right.

Sally excused herself from the table. On the way to the lavatory she passed the beautiful young man in the charcoal jacket. She noticed his eyes of softest hazel framed with dusty lashes as he helped his tearstained girlfriend into a black astrakhan coat. The woman looked older close up, almost as ancient as Gregory, and Sally thought about the injustice of it all, of what life had awarded her while the crying woman got the top prize. Such a beautiful young man. She saw his silky grey scarf fall to the floor as she passed through the cloakroom and pushed open the door marked with a curlicued 'F'. She sat on the lavatory for a long time, feet up on the seat, head cradled on her knees.

At times like these she was reminded of herself as a

child. It was like the time her parents had moved house and she had lain in her new bedroom in the strangeness of the despised new home and shut her eyes tight, willing the move to be a dream, convincing herself that when she opened them again, everything would be as it had been, that the familiar chestnut tree would once again be brushing its leaves against her window. But it never worked then, and it didn't work now. When she opened her eyes, she was still in the restaurant, and she knew that Gregory, and not a beautiful young man with warm hazel eyes, was waiting for her at their table.

On her way back through the cloakroom, she noticed the silky grey scarf still lying where the young man had dropped it. She picked it up and held it briefly to her face. It smelt of summer and limes and she knew she had to keep it. With an infidel's stealth she rolled it into a ball and dropped it into her handbag.

'Are you all right?' asked Gregory, predictably, when she sat, once more, at their corner table. 'I've ordered sticky toffee pudding and two spoons but tell them quick if you would like something else.' Sally thought sticky toffee pudding would be about as meaningful as anything else at this stage of her life.

Later still, in bed, Sally lay with her hand beneath her pillow, stroking the silky grey scarf, imagining the smell of summer and limes infusing her body and picturing a tousled dark head next to her. When Gregory turned to her, she saw his eyes as soft hazel, just for a moment, before they faded before her to watery grey in the half-light.

'Mmm. Did you enjoy that as much as I did?' he asked.

'Yes. It was great,' she said, letting her hand slip from beneath the pillow and her soft secret. As her mother said, she had made her bed. And now she was lying in it.

The Mermaid's Purse

The boy with the warm hazel eyes imagines himself in the spotlight. He feels conspicuous, burning red, as though the eyes of the other diners scorch him.

'Oh God,' he says when she tells him that she is pregnant. 'What are you going to do?'

'Do?' says Leoni. 'What do you mean, *do*?'

He watches her as she peels wax like rolling tears from the wine bottle candlestick. He sees her quick fingers moulding the wax, bonier than he had ever noticed. The bluish veins and tendons twitch beneath translucent veal skin, thinner over the knuckles.

He thinks about pretty Charlotte, his girlfriend. What will he tell her this time? He thinks about Charlotte's back that arches like a drawn bow, and then turns away from him when she sleeps. Charlotte's back. Honey-coloured, smooth, like silk that has been ironed.

'I'm not really father material,' he says, sounding like a sulky teenager who has been caught red-handed at some misdemeanour or other. A baby! What will he tell his parents? His mother doesn't seem like grandmother material yet either.

Charlotte will slap his face, like she did once before and swore never to do again. 'Next time, I'll go,' she said, rubbing her hand and shaking.

Not father material. Leoni sighs, she doesn't know Len well enough to argue.

'Are you sure? Are you definitely pregnant?'

'I did the test this morning.' Leoni knew, a woman's instinct, the moment the pregnancy tester turned pink, that Len would be out of her life. But she had made a pact with herself. She wanted a man and she wanted a baby, but at her age not necessarily in that order.

Leoni nods her head, still looking down at the pearly wax that she is rolling between her fingers. For his sake, she stifles a smile. 'Yes, I am sure. I'm having a baby.'

She looks at Len, untouchable now across the expanse of pink linen tablecloth, and back to the warm wax in her hands. He really is just a boy, she thinks, and she a fully grown woman. She can hear the clinking of cutlery and murmured conversation from the neighbouring tables but notices none of the other diners. Len looks at her over his hands, which he has pressed into either side of his face, pushing the skin tight up to his temples and stretching his eyes to the sides of his head. Like a shark, thinks Leoni, seeing him panicked and writhing on the deck.

No, this isn't fair on him, she decides, as she knew she would; she should let him off the hook. Her mouth tastes salty. She takes a gulp from her water glass.

'Of course,' she says, fighting with herself, 'the baby might not be yours at all.'

Len throws his body against the back of his chair; his shoulders visibly drop as she cuts him free.

'Oh God,' he says, meeting her eyes. 'Oh God, you mean this? The baby isn't mine?'

'I don't know.'

'It's not mine, is it?'

He really is a child, she thinks. He is beseeching her to reassure him. To tell him something that she cannot know herself.

'I thought you slept with that guy from Boston. That writer. You did, didn't you?'

The waiter is approaching. Len is looking so relieved that Leoni thinks he might start announcing details of her sex life to the entire restaurant.

'Shhh,' she says. 'Shut up!'

'Let's just have a main course and get out of here,' Len suggests, as the waiter stands, notebook poised. He's not even giving me the time for dinner, Leoni thinks, he wants out.

'I'll just have the Dover sole then.'

'Yes, I'll have the sole too,' says Len, staring into the distance, towards the restaurant door. He can't look at the menu, he won't look at Leoni.

Yes, she spent two days with the screenwriter, she tells him. And then there's Paul. She has been sleeping with Paul for ages, on and off, mainly because she feels sorry for him. She first slept with him years before the brain tumour that left him unable to control the muscles on the left side of his face. Not that it made any difference; it was just that he was so bitter about the blow that life had dealt him that no one else would take him on.

And then there was that shameful evening with Clara's Robert. Clara always says that Leoni is trouble, but she doesn't know the half of it. They have been friends for most of their lives. Leoni remembers stealing brandy from outside the home economics department at school and Clara taking the rap with her. Leoni found the quarter of Hennessy in one of the third-former's tupperware containers – they were making Christmas cakes – and took it out to the red-brick bunker outside the biology lab where she and Clara, and Pete and Ian, the Downey twins, swigged it while the broken old crow, the unofficial school mascot, hopped furiously up and down in its wire net enclosure. Both girls french-kissed both twins to see if they kissed the same. 'It was a scientific experiment,' Leoni tried to explain. But they all got detention and letters home just the same.

Clara's mum told Clara to have nothing to do with Leoni for a while after that. This was quite easy, as Leoni was suspended for the rest of the term for robbing the school nativity scene, leaving a ransom note demanding a fiver for the safe return of the Infant Jesus.

But Clara is still her best friend, even now. Some friend Leoni has turned out to be. She cannot explain, even to herself, through her shame, how she ended up with Robert, Clara's husband, in her bed.

But he was so very careful, thank goodness. Even as she lay there, her body pulsating, desperate, at that moment, for him to stay deep inside her, preferably forever, he pulled out. He was still above her. She started to cry. 'I didn't know if you were on the pill or not,' he said. Sensible Robert. Oh, Clara.

On the scale of probability, Leoni reckons, the father of her baby is almost certainly Len. Irresistible Len – 'My very first toyboy,' she told Clara – with his curly hair and his moody black and white landscapes pegged up like washing, developing in the womby red glow of his darkroom.

Len with the strong wrists below the frayed edges of his black jumper. The wrists, his hands on the steering wheel as he drove his wicked older woman to Wales, to his flat above the beach near Cardiff. From his balcony they watched the surfers riding the waves, black wetsuits with neon stripes, twisting and turning astride the rearing sea, swooping down, careering, impossibly still standing, skimming like stones across the water towards the beach.

Drinking vodka and grapefruit juice, playing home, Leoni and Len watched the sun set over the sea and wandered down the pebble path to the beach below. They walked barefoot in the shallows, picking up stones and throwing them into the sea. White moonstones, bouncing across the black water, then swallowed by waves.

'Look at this,' said Leoni, holding a tiny black envelope. 'A mermaid's purse.' It rattled when she shook it. 'Shark eggs!' she said. Shark eggs wrapped in armour like hardened tar, for safe keeping. Then, in the grip of madness, she removed her clothes and ran into the night-black sea, throwing her moon-silvered body into the waves, which hurled her back to Len on the shore in a swirl of sand and foam. He was shouting from the beach, 'Only you!'

A wave as big as a house sucked her inside and she tumbled around and around, salt water rushing through her, and then the sea flung her back out of the foam and high on to the beach, gasping and grazed, her hair like snakes around her face. 'Only you,' said Len, again, running to her. 'Only you would do something like that!' And she lay there on the sand, washed up at his feet. Afterwards, they sat on his balcony, Leoni wrapped in his quilt. She hadn't bathed and she crossed and uncrossed her legs, enjoying the sticky trail and the sand on her thighs.

There is just a shiny fish skeleton, cartoon-like in its completeness, and a wedge of lemon left on Len's plate. He has dissected, cut and swallowed his sole in the time that it has taken Leoni to eat just a couple of mouthfuls of her fish.

'I want this baby, Len,' says Leoni, as she pours more water into her glass. 'I'm not expecting anything from you.'

'But what if I am the father, what then?' Len is dabbing furiously at his mouth with the pink napkin. 'You can't do this to me,' he says. 'I just hope it's not mine.'

Leoni knows that he has the honesty of a child but his words make her buckle somewhere inside, like a punch in the stomach. In the fairy tale of her mind, before this evening, she allowed herself to see him elated, enveloping her in warm arms. 'This was meant to be!' said the fairy-tale Len.

'I'm so sorry,' she says as her eyes brim, 'I seem to be getting overemotional.' (*Overemotional!* This could be the father of my child, she thinks.) 'It must be the hormones kicking in.'

The waiter removes the plates. He stares at Leoni's unfinished sole, his face a picture of forced concern, a question. 'I think there's been a mistake,' she mouths. 'I want to eat Dover coal, not Dover sole.'

'I beg your pardon?' The waiter is irritated. This table was booked for dinner, not a quick course, he feels like telling them. And not even a decent bottle of wine. If he drank that stuff, he'd get a roaring hangover.

'Nothing. This was perfect, wonderful, it's just that I'm pregnant. I'm eschewing for two,' says Leoni, not looking at the food, not looking at the waiter, not smiling.

She is glad to see that Len doesn't laugh. At last he reaches across the table and takes her hand. He doesn't like how it feels but forces himself to hold it.

'Do you mind if I tell you what I think?' he says.

'Go on,' says Leoni, but she already knows what he thinks by the way he is holding her hand. It feels as though he would like to shake it, like someone in business, concluding a deal.

'I know it's hard at your age, but I think you should have an abortion. It's not fair on this child. It's not fair if it doesn't even know who its father is. And if it is me, well, we're hardly a steady relationship. What are you going to tell it?'

'Len,' she says, pulling her fingers away from his, 'you don't have to be in my life. No hard feelings, eh? What I tell my child will be my business entirely.'

Leoni and Len part in the taxi as she drops him off at Paddington station. They have barely spoken since they left the restaurant. They stood like strangers, flagging down taxis. They only share one because they happen to be going in the same direction.

'So, I just go back to Cardiff now, is that it?' says Len, as they draw ever closer to the station. Leoni is counting the seconds; she knows that she will not see him again once he is on that train. The fantasy voice insists that there is still time for him to change his mind; the cool voice knows that he will not. A baby was never part of *his* fantasy. Stockings were. Moonlight and beaches. And the geographical distance between them, that was part of his fantasy too. She can see clearly now and the station is in sight. As the driver pulls in, their fingertips touch briefly.

'What can I say?' he says as he pulls open the door. 'Shall I give you something for the taxi?'

Leoni almost laughs then. 'No, you don't need to give me anything,' she says, and watches him as he stumbles like a giddy child, across the road and out of sight.

★

Leoni talks to her baby throughout her pregnancy. 'Your daddy was a wonderful man!' She becomes more and more impatient with this fiction as the baby grows. She wants quite desperately to know who has fathered her child.

She talks to other women at the antenatal clinic; it *is* exciting, like waiting nine months to open a present, they all agree. Or to taste a new recipe. A bun in the oven! Only in her case she hasn't the faintest idea of what to expect, because half of the ingredients are still a mystery to her. She is impatient for her baby to be born, and anxious to see the features that will reveal the truth. In her mind she tries casting Paul and the American, but mostly Len, in the role of her child's father, but her mind refuses to play. 'Sperm donor, sperm donor,' corrects a voice in her head. 'The biological father,' says Clara. 'Don't you think the baby will want to know its biological father?'

Leoni knows that labour has started. It is dark outside. It is raining steadily and there is condensation on the windows. She moves to the bathroom and runs a bath. Adds rose and geranium. The water foams. She looks with amazement down at her stomach, rising out of the water, round, glistening, and then pulled fully square and hard by the muscles surrounding the baby. She lies in the bath and dreams of the sea.

She is losing track of time. The bath is tepid now. She puts her head right under the water and empties her lungs, rising up as each contraction peaks, then silence. She is drunk, floating on endorphins as her body softens once again. She thinks about the surfers and rides each wave, twisting her body, taking the full thrust, determined not to be knocked over as the force peaks, then soaring down towards the lull and waiting for the next wave, and the next.

She is out of the bath, dripping pools at her feet. She is walking up and down from window to bed, bed to window, concentrating on the lines on the carpet, curling into a ball and falling to the floor sometimes as the force within grips her, holding it, flowing towards the next moment of calm when she is back on her feet and marching again. She watches the second hand on the clock, counts as it passes twelve. It goes around the clock six times exactly before the next contraction starts. She hasn't the faintest idea what the time is; it is only the minutes that interest her.

She waits until another contraction has peaked and then calls a taxi. 'Come on. Come on!' The telephone rings for such a long time; she must get the words out, her address, before the next wave strikes. She calls the hospital. 'It's started, I'm on my way.'

'I must get dressed, I must get dressed now.' She struggles into her clothes that are lying in a heap by the bath, soaked from the water that has sloshed everywhere. 'Where are my shoes?' She can't think where anything is as another surge comes crashing through her body. She knows that she should have gone in before this.

The driver is ringing the bell. Leoni looks at the clock; insanely she calculates that if she waits until another contraction strikes, and if he takes the direct route, she will make it to the hospital without alarming him too much.

She summons all her strength and opens the door. The driver takes one look at this woman with streaming hair and wet clothes and knows what is happening. 'I can't take you, you must call an ambulance,' he says.

Leoni is standing on the doorstep. 'Please,' she says, and then she is tugging at his sleeve as the pain starts building within her and her knees buckle.

'Come on, back inside. I'll call the hospital for you.' The driver half-lifts, half-pushes her back through the door. 'Now, which hospital? Tell me who to call. For Christ's sake.' Leoni is rolling from side to side, her eyes shut. She tells him the name of the hospital. 'I can't deliver a baby,' he says as he flings himself across the room to her telephone. 'Where's your husband? Shall I call him? He should be here.'

The midwife is on the phone. The driver feels he can't leave but he doesn't want to touch this flailing, wailing woman. The contractions leave no time for conversation. 'You stay there,' the midwife says. 'We'll send someone to you.'

Leoni cannot move from the spot in the hallway, where she tries to stagger to her feet but is knocked down again by the force. Somehow, crawling now, she makes it back to the bathroom and throws up into the lavatory. The driver stands outside the bathroom door, praying loudly to the heavens.

The driver shoots from the hall when the ambulance

arrives. 'Blimey!' he says to the midwife. 'That was a close call. If it's a boy, make sure she calls him Sam after me, won't you? Honestly, people. And no bleeding husband anywhere to be seen.' The midwife takes one look at Leoni and knows that this will be a home birth.

The midwife is running water into the bath. 'Would you like to get into the tub?'

Leoni hears the words but they mean nothing. She knows she has to respond as she grips the corner of the bath. 'Yes,' she says, meaning, 'I don't know.' She can't move from where she is. There is such a pressure bearing down, she feels like her insides will explode as she crouches there. It has been three minutes since help arrived but it feels like seconds. Or hours. 'I want to push.'

'Well,' says the midwife, 'you had better take off your knickers.'

The midwife helps her to remove her pants; she is still dressed in her skirt and jumper. Another huge contraction sends her diving down, deep inside herself, as the midwife presses her fingers into the base of her back.

Then she pushes herself into the wave roaring in her ears; it sounds like her own voice screaming but it is coming from across a valley and echoing back at her. Once more and then a starburst of holly-berry red spatters the towels beneath her feet. 'The head is coming,' says the midwife. Another wave and this time Leoni can hear another voice but closer than her own. She can feel the vibrations of crying, as the baby's head is born, and then, with another push, her child is free of her body. Leoni is holding her baby in her arms. Slippery mermaid baby, hands grasping at fistfuls of air and trying to make sense of the cool lightness slipping through her fingers.

'Have I had my baby?' Leoni is blinded as she emerges from the tunnel, triumphant, holding a new person in her arms.

The midwife laughs. 'A beautiful girl. Yes.'

Ten tiny doll's fingers, opening and closing, lost in space. 'A girl!' Leoni's eyes are locked into her daughter's gaze for the first time. Deep into eyes of every colour in the world, beneath a high brow and a shock of wet dark hair. The baby girl looks so surprised as she stares at Leoni, it is as though she has opened a present. 'Oh look,' she seems to say, 'a mother, just what I wanted.'

Leoni laughs as she holds her daughter in her arms, tears streaming down her cheeks. 'Who are you?' she whispers, but as she says it she realises that she knows this person, has always known her. She just hasn't met her until now. And the father of her baby? It hasn't crossed her mind to wonder.

'Here you are. Don't cry, my baby. Oh, don't cry. I love you, I love you. I love you!'

Daddy's Girl

Shapes in the night. Monochrome to the eye but coloured in by the mind's eye in a familiar room. On the back of the door hangs her dressing gown; cherry-red, once fluffy, now turned bobbly with wear. Beneath it, her first party dress, midnight-blue velvet with a puritan lace collar and a tiny jacket with the hallmarked silver buttons that spell her name as they fasten down – E at the collar, M, I, L, and Y at the waist – each hand-crafted by the silversmith who had lived at the end of the lane. On her bedside table a maplewood frame holding a photograph of a five-year-old Emily wearing the dress. A little girl with a heart-shaped face, laughing at the camera, seated on her father's knee. His face romanesque in profile, as he apparently whispers something into his daughter's ear. A sweet something, no doubt, as sweet nothings are not part of his repertoire.

Later, the womb light of the dawn will filter through the crushed raspberry silk curtains and Popinjay, Emily's Siamese cat (a surprise present from her father on her last birthday and a perfect replica of the Popinjay who went before), will oil his way silently on to the sleeping girl's pillow. But right now, she drifts on her waterbed, swaddled in blankets, the silken corner of one pressed against her cheek, not so much a security blanket as a life raft.

Marooned on the other side of the bed is her husband. Awake again, limbs reaching across the ocean of the bed towards her, rebuffed in no uncertain terms earlier: 'No, not now, Richard,' she said. 'But Emily we're in bed,' he pleaded, 'it's Saturday night, if not now, then when?' How he hated sounding like a sex maniac. Her eyes were bleary; he suspected that parts of her body were, in any case, already asleep. She enveloped herself in the bedclothes, hugging her pillow to her chest. 'I'm so tired, please don't make me feel bad.'

Richard is left wondering if he dares take the matter into his own hands. As usual, he decides against solo action as the damned bed, one of Emily's father's many thoughtful presents, might betray his stealth, swirling up a storm and possibly leaving him shipwrecked in the spare room.

On his bedside table is a matching maplewood frame with his favourite photograph. It is of Emily and himself waving from a beribboned car as they depart for their honeymoon. It was not this photograph that appeared in the newspaper when they married, of course. No, he hadn't figured in that one at all; rather, a paparazzi shot of Emily

arriving at the church on her father's arm had found its way
into the social column beneath the headline: 'The playwright's daughter weds.' He wouldn't have minded quite so
much had this little item not appeared in the very newspaper where he worked as a reporter. No mention was made,
of course, of *his* father, a civil engineer. Note that 'a', for,
short of committing armed robbery, there is small chance
of his ever becoming *the* civil engineer. A bit like Richard
himself really; *a* journalist and sometime book reviewer,
whose hopes of becoming *the* writer and critic whilst com-
posing 800-word court reports about old ladies stealing
pork chops, or 'This Week's Paperbacks' for the book
pages, afford him little opportunity of becoming anything
with a *the* other than, perhaps, *the* hack son-in-law of
Britain's greatest living playwright.

And tomorrow, Britain's greatest living playwright
will be coming to stay. This is probably the reason, Richard
thinks, that Emily has been so especially off sex, off colour
and off in a world of her own all week. Why, she was actually physically sick yesterday.

They were fixing up the spare room together, making
it fit for Emily's father:

'Blimey, Emily, can we afford these?' he said, as Emily
unwrapped new white linen sheets.

'Probably not,' she replied, crumpling the cellophane
into a ball, 'but the old ones were the orange ones which
went with your old duvet and I just couldn't picture Daddy
enjoying his sleep in *those*.'

He was scrubbing at a pungent circle of stains in the

carpet at the time (he had long suspected that the wretched Popinjay used this room as a urinal when it was raining or cold outside, and, on moving a chest of drawers, this suspicion had been revealed in all its horrible sodden accuracy).

'I don't remember my sheets being orange,' he objected. 'They were more of a terracotta, and anyway, I never heard you complain about my damn sheets when you stayed with me then.'

Emily wrinkled her nose. 'They *were* orange, and that was then.' Her jaw was set. Richard didn't know what she meant by 'that was then'.

The worst of the mess was cleared up, but he was still busy with a scrubbing brush and a plastic bowl of hot water and Domestos. He was about to pick a fight, and could feel the blood rushing to his head, when he noticed that Emily had turned as white as the linen. She flung down the sheets and started retching into the basin. A bit rich that, he thought, when he was the one dealing with the disgusting habits of her cat. But he removed his rubber gloves, rubbed her back and when she stopped heaving and started to sob, told her to try not to get so worked up about her father's visit.

It has been a long and rather shocking absence though, he has to admit. Until the day of their wedding, as far as he knows, there were few days in Emily's life that she had not spent at least part of with her father. And attached father and daughter remained, even after she found a place for Richard; initially in her bed, then in her life and finally, so she said, in her heart. After college each day, Emily visited her father to play games. Backgammon, chess and draughts. Games for two. Later in the evening she would meet Richard, her lovesick swain, for altogether different games. Played out beneath his terracotta duvet, this was a completely new and adventurous sort of activity for two, which she accepted as readily as her father's kisses. And now this same girl sleeps beside him, tired of his games, her back curved in a sickle of rejection.

I must have been a fool to imagine it could have been different, he thinks churlishly, as he lies in the dark. It was not as if people hadn't tried to warn him as he skipped about, confident that she would, indeed, one day be his.

'Are you sure he's going to let you marry her?' said old Jake Selzer, the cynical theatre critic who shared his desk at the newspaper. 'I can't imagine he thinks you nearly good enough for his little princess.'

'Thanks, Jake,' said Richard. 'It's good to know that I'm so highly regarded. Get your own bloody coffee in future.'

'Come now, Richard,' said Jake, stirring two saccharine pills into the styrofoam cup. 'It's not you. It would be anyone. That man has brought up his girl single-handed. No nannies, no housekeepers, nothing. Just the two of them. You know that.'

Of course Richard knew that well. Everyone spoke as glowingly of his fiancée's father's extraordinary parental prowess as they did of his plays: he had been mother and confidant as well as father to the girl. 'A marvellous example to all other single parents,' or so everyone said. Oh yes, and he had been playmate and idol too, Richard knew that from his own observations and later from Emily herself.

'Have you really never ever hated your father, not even one little bit?' he once asked, as they shared a Saturday-night post-coital bar of Cadbury's Whole Nut beneath the terracotta duvet.

'Good heavens, why do you ask that?' said Emily, surprised.

'It's just that I always thought it was a normal part of growing up. You must know how it's supposed to be: all that adolescent fury that goes hand in hand with despising your parents, hating their clothes, slamming doors, having accidents in their cars, that sort of thing.'

Emily was smiling at him. 'You might think so,' she said, 'but it just doesn't seem remotely normal to me. I can't even imagine hating Daddy. If you think that's odd, then so be it.'

'OK, well maybe "hate" is too strong a word,' he conceded. 'Howsabout just irritated a little bit? Surely he must have irked you at some point in your life.'

'Sorry to disappoint you, but no, Daddy has never irritated me at all,' she said. 'You are though, so take this and shut up.' And she plunged her hands between his legs, her mouth chocolatey on his. He gave up the conversation – with pleasure.

Richard may have acted hurt when old Jake Selzer questioned him, but he had to admit that he had been more than a little surprised, in fact, when the great man acquiesced with seeming ease to his request to marry his daughter. It was strange how he could recall the day of his proposal more for the conversation he had with her father than for that with Emily herself. He remembered doing the whole red roses bit and being on bended knee and feeling hot with embarrassment. He remembered Emily's hand on his shoulder and looking up into her faraway eyes from his position on the bedroom carpet, but he couldn't for the life of him recall what she had actually replied, only that it was neither a firm 'yes' or a 'no', more of a noncommittal shrug with a smile – or was it a laugh? – and some sort of suggestion that he should ask her father for her hand.

Two hours later he found himself, with growling stomach and sweating palms, knocking on the front door of the great man's house in Oxfordshire, Emily by his side, prettier than ever in a long cotton dress printed all over with rosebuds.

Once inside the oak-beamed kitchen, he came straight to the point, as Emily's father, with a wink to his daughter, set the bottle of chilled Krug that he'd brought – 'Something to celebrate, eh, Richard?' – into a bucket of ice.

'Oh, I do hope so,' Richard replied, and then, 'I know you might think it a bit soon, or that Emily should finish her studies first,' his words sounding like the well-rehearsed speech that indeed they were, 'but I was wondering if you would consider allowing me to marry her. I love her so much, you see.'

Emily's father ground the bottle into the ice and looked quizzically at his daughter, who was flushed as pink as the roses on her dress. She gave a small nod and bit her bottom lip. Her father, still silent, reached into a glass-fronted cupboard and removed three long-stemmed glasses, placing them beside the champagne. Wordlessly, he pulled out the bottle, untwisted the wire cradle from the cork and wound a blue checked tea towel around the neck. He eased out the cork, which made a 'fuff' noise rather than a pop, poured three glasses and, gesturing to Richard and Emily to take their glasses, raised his a full arm's length to the ceiling. 'To my daughter and her betrothed. I wish you all the happiness that is possible in this odd little world in which we find ourselves.' They all three clinked glasses. Emily's eyes were overflowing as her father and Richard drank their champagne.

And now look where it's got me, I might as well spend my life with a ghost in a chastity belt. Richard doesn't always feel so resentful but as any insomniac knows, the night is a bitter place. In the morning, when he awakes, he will, he knows, once again feel sympathy for his child-like bride. It was as though by marrying him she had been orphaned.

Since the tragedy at her birth, Emily's father had seen to it that her life was free of all the usual twentieth-century trauma; filled, as it had been, with hair ribbons and satin sashes, books by Laura Ingalls-Wilder and Arthur Ransome, ponies and flower gardens, magicians on her birthday. Later it was art galleries and operas, antique fountain pens and perfect strings of pearls presented in turquoise satin boxes over tea at Fortnum's. Always at Fortnum's, and always something to celebrate, for Emily shone at school. Her father saw it as his job to ensure that no door was ever closed to her. Emily still believed in Father Christmas at the age of ten.

Life changed when the newly-weds returned, thinner but browner, from their honeymoon. It was then that Emily discovered the sad fact that, as is often the case in adulthood, for every door that opens, another closes. While they were away, Emily's father developed romantic notions of his own. He became entangled with a Japanese woman who painted pictures of Mount Fuji from memory. By the time Emily and Richard returned from India he had all but disappeared to further their acquaintance in a disused light-house – to which no telephone engineer had ever been invited – perched at the edge of the Atlantic in southern Ireland.

The hours slip by in the blackness of his dreamless night. Richard's mind wanders to a winter Wednesday, the February before the wedding, and the first moment he set eyes on Emily. A walk on Primrose Hill with his sister, both shivering as fresh snowflakes, as large and soft as butterfly wings, whispered to the trodden night's fall, which was already streaked with brown and corrugated in places by the early-morning sledges of schoolchildren. The trees like twisted ironwork against the cold steel sky, the entire hill hushed as London sighed, its traffic easing through the slush. The only other sound came from the two strangers, there, down the hill, at the children's swings. A couple: the man pushing the woman, who squealed as the creaking chains jerked the seat higher and higher. Richard watched with his sister from the top of the hill, hearing the woman's laughter, begging her companion to stop. When the man finally did allow the swing to dwindle, she jumped down and scooping some snow from the slide, hurled it at him. Soon they were running and shrieking, out of the children's play area and up the hill, through the now swarming snow. They slowed, arm in arm, still laughing, as they reached their clandestine audience of two. The woman, he could see, had snow on her lashes; the man was much older, much colder, as his daughter greeted Richard's sister, recognising her from college. They all four went for frothy hot chocolate and apple strudel in the Polish café across the road.

He looks again at the wedding picture in the half-light before the dawn. Emily's smile. She hasn't smiled like that since. When they got back from India, he carried her over the threshold – every bit the amorous husband. He almost tripped on a pile of post, mainly brown envelopes and colourful flyers about a new takeaway pizza parlour, as he hurried for the bedroom. But Emily spotted the smooth manila envelope, and instantly recognised the fine black ink script. The word 'Personal', so unnecessary in the top left corner, and, he thought, its contents so cruelly timed. 'Welcome back,' her father's letter began. 'The house seems too empty without you and I am being comforted by a friend (of the female persuasion) here, by the sea.' He went on to give his address in Ireland, to eulogise about the positive effects of the negative ions he was breathing and to wish his 'newly married lassie' well. He said that he would be in touch when he felt 'stronger'.

To find her father suddenly absent, an ocean between them, was a shock to the girl, everyone agreed. After all, this man, throughout her twenty-three years, had been almost as famous for his stubborn celibacy – a matter of much interest, or so it appeared, to readers of women's magazines – as he was in less frivolous circles for his plays.

From that day, Emily, who had always smelled of warm vanilla, took to the bathroom, scrubbing herself livid in steaming baths – sometimes several in a single day – to emerge hot and sad and smelling of Cussons Imperial Leather. To the outside world – or what she saw of it, anyway – she affected not to mind. She hoped he was happy in Ireland, she said, and spent the intervening months immersed in her thesis and Lawrence Durrell, surfacing occasionally to send her errant father small jars of Patum Peperium and pots of Trumper's lavender shaving cream, accompanied by comical postcards of gargoyles or pigs. Once, while staying with his parents in Kent, Richard had stolen a look at one of the postcards, hoping for a clue as to how she was really coping. It was a picture of the local clock tower. On the reverse it said simply: 'For Civil Engineers, look in Yellow Pages under Boring.' He forgave her snobbish snipe at his father almost instantly when she emerged, pink as a sugar shrimp, from the scalding bath.

He still cannot sleep. The bed amplifies his discomfort, water lapping against rubber as he turns back and forth, to and fro, facing Emily and then the wall. He looks at the clock and calculates that it is just six hours and thirty-three minutes until Britain's greatest living playwright will touch down at the airport; an hour more by taxi, and father and daughter will be reunited. His neck aches and he realises that his jaw muscles are too tense for sleep. It isn't just the lack of sex that is causing this insomnia, he realises. It is more the fear of finding himself an unwilling goose-berry, squashed by father and daughter at the moment of impact.

The Japanese painter is history, he knows. 'Hands fluttering over my body like cold little fishes,' was what Emily's father wrote to describe what, he claimed, were her fruitless efforts to seduce him over those months in the lonely tower. He wonders why Emily's father should feel so keen to clear his name of any sexual contact with the woman. After all, it would hardly be an act of impropriety for a fifty-six-year-old widower to have sex with a willing and consenting adult.

As he lies listening to Emily's breathing, he admits to himself how disappointed he is by her father's apparent lack of libido. His biggest fear is about to come true, and suddenly he knows what causes this and so many other sleepless nights: with Emily's father off screwing in Ireland for the foreseeable future – as he had assumed he was – she might not have been the most spirited company, but she had been his. Now the marriage is to become overpopulated again. He knows that he is going to have this out with Emily – and her father too if necessary – but before he does, he will leave the flat and allow them to have some time together. He will buy lunch. Japanese lunch, he thinks, wickedly. At last, he sleeps.

Emily is still in the bathroom when he leaves so he takes the opportunity to kick the cat off the sofa on the way out. He feels remarkably cheerful as he calls to her that he will buy something special for lunch and leave her to welcome her father ('the returning Casanova' is what he calls him) in peace.

Driving up the Edgware Road he whistles along to Gloria Gaynor on the radio. 'I Will Survive': a fine omen, he thinks. His new resolve to make his feelings clear is cheering him up no end. The Japanese lunch will help, of that he feels sure. He smiles to himself. Emily is a kind girl, an intelligent girl. She will see that a married couple need a life of their own, just as her father should have a life of his own too. He is thinking of a holiday in the Canary Isles, just the two of them. Get some winter sun. Surprise her. Come back. New job on different newspaper. Arts correspondent, something like that. Father-in-law could pull a few strings. Cottage in the country. Two babies, a girl and a boy. Father-in-law visiting for Sunday lunch, say, twice a month. He pulls into the multistorey car park and finds a space just across from the entrance to the food store at Yoahan Plaza. Another good omen.

He walks into the hall, grabbing a blue plastic basket, passing the gaudy New Year Wishing Dolls, the Mongolian cooking pots, the fortune cookies and rice crackers. He practically skips through the aisles while a Japanese version of Peters and Lee plays over the tannoy, picking a large greenish-white daikon radish because, in his new-found enthusiasm, he simply likes the look of it. He adds green tea bags, a large boxed bottle of sake, some packets of dried miso soup. He is tempted by the red and white octopus tentacles with their black-ringed suckers but resists at the thought of Emily's face should she happen upon them in the fridge. Before he makes his way to the blue-tiled take-away sushi bar, he stops off at the adjoining café for a sashimi breakfast of squid and uni (described in the menu as 'challenging'), served in the shadow of a large tower of red and pink paper lanterns and giant Hitachi TV screens showing the news of snow in Tokyo. At the formica-topped table opposite is a small Japanese doll of a girl, about two years old, with a face of Victorian porcelain and blue Mickey Mouse wellingtons which she kicks over the edge of her highchair. Her father feeds her seaweed-wrapped prawns as he keeps one eye on the television screens.

He checks the time. Emily and her father will be embracing about now. He gulps down the rest of the raw squid and the sticky Caramac-coloured strips of sea urchin eggs, smiles at the child and continues with his plastic basket to the takeaway sushi bar.

For Emily, he chooses two boxes of her favourite tekka maki; each raw tuna slice succulent as rare steak in its roll of plump sticky rice and seaweed jacket. For her father he selects sushi: six pieces of the challenging uni, six pieces of impossibly orange salmon, four bundles of cooked egg strips bound together by black strips of seaweed, some sliced raw octopus and four more pieces of sushi glistening with amber beads of salmon roe. Together with the dayglo-green pyramid of wasabi, the pink sliced ginger and the serrated-edged oba leaf decoration, it makes, so he thinks, a most *interesting*-looking lunch. It is time to reclaim the hand of his wife.

The door to the flat is open, the hallway awash with his father-in-law's blue and green canvas bags. From the kitchen he can hear laughter. He can smell cooking. He stands in the doorway, drops his carrier bags to the floor. Father and daughter both jump when they see him. His father-in-law has grown a beard. Emily is wearing her new pale-blue cashmere cardigan. Britain's greatest living play-wright stands, hugs him, beard scratchy, thanks him for taking such good care of his daughter while he was away. Writing a new play, he says. Emily confesses that she *made* her father cook the moment he arrived. She has *so* missed his macaroni cheese. She sits between them; her cardigan matches her eyes exactly. The macaroni cheese is just how she likes it: with parsley and crunchy bacon topping. She takes one of Richard's hands in her right hand, her father's in her left. She stares at the steaming Pyrex dish set in the middle of the table, still holding Richard's hand in the way that one holds a banister.

She does not look at her husband when she speaks, but turns her face to her father. 'Daddy,' she says, her voice trembling now, 'you are going to be a grandfather.'

Blood Roses
in the Snow

'Excuse me, Mrs McCluskie, I think you know why we are here.' The policeman has a search warrant and is standing on the doorstep with a young policewoman and another woman who I recognise as the brisk social worker who busied herself rearranging my life several moons ago. Her voice is deliberately sweet, hiding a centre as hard as nut brittle. 'Elaine,' she says, 'I think you had better let us in.'

I am not surprised to see them, I have been expecting them for some time. I have played and replayed this scene to myself each night, though I have tried not to let it upset me. I have tried to live for the present and the softness of my love. But I have always known that sooner or later they would be here to rob me of my baby, to take you, my precious darling, away and out into the cold world. They are here now and my heart silently breaks before them. They are standing on the doorstep and soon they will go, taking away the thing that is most precious to me. I tip over the terracotta pot in which the snowdrops are flowering before I let them in, spilling on to the snow, peat and gravel and the small plants that had been flourishing, as a warning to Hugh not to come near. At least I manage that, and for a moment I feel quite proud of my composure, of how, at this terrible moment, I am true to my word. I promised him that I would leave this signal to protect him, should the time come when he too would be in danger. I will not see him again, in all probability, but that isn't what matters now.

They are in the sitting room now, their horrid shiny shoes have left a trail of dirty marks across the new carpet. 'Elaine, where is the baby?' asks the social worker, holding my hands as I sit on the sofa, beseeching cow's eyes locked into mine. She speaks again, disguising the hard edges of her voice with a mock compassion. 'Elaine, you must tell us where the baby is.'

You are having your morning nap, curled around your favourite fluffy dog, your thumb resting on your bottom lip beneath the curve of your cheek, soft and flushed as a ripe peach, breathing softly in your cot. You are too young to appreciate your cot but I have to admit it is a masterpiece. It took me three months to paint. First, I had to strip it of the shop's polyurethane finish before I gave it a cool-green colourwash. All the animals that I painted, I copied from postcards that I have been collecting for years in preparation.

There are lambs gambolling on the headboard in a field of lush spring grass, and four tabby kittens and a golden retriever puppy sitting before a roaring log fire to watch over you from the other end. On each of the bars I painted buttercups and twining honeysuckle and blackberries that look ripe enough for picking.

It is so sad that you will never sleep in this little cot again. You will never look at the lambs that I painted and say, 'Baa baa,' or get to name the puppy and the kittens, or give each one a goodnight kiss before I tuck you in, covering you with the soft ivory blanket that I knitted in pearly moss-stitch, the silky edge of the ribbon that I sewed around the border familiar to your plump cheek. I will make sure that the fluffy dog goes with you but I know that they won't let you keep it for long. It will go in the dustbin along with any lingering memories you might have of me.

I wish I could escape for long enough to take you once again into my arms but the policeman is blocking the door. I want to nuzzle into the top of your head and breathe in the toasty-buttered-currant-bun smell of you. I want to feel your face resting against my chest, your fingers curled tightly around my thumb, and then gaze at you once more before I drown in the deep blue eyes that I will never look into again.

There is so much I want to tell you before they take you away. The day we came home together was the happiest of my life. Just the sight of you washed away the years of melancholy and yearning. You filled the emptiness and

made me sing. 'Roses are red, dilly dilly, violets are blue,' I
crooned while I rocked you in my arms before the fire. I
think of you, now, after that first bath, your perfect pink
body swaddled in the softest towel, your eyes peeping out
from the white folds into mine and the heat of my love
engulfing us both, keeping you warm and safe as I held you
against me.

By bedtime you were so tearful that it made my poor
heart ache as you sobbed, turning your face this way and
that in your beautiful new cot. I wound up the little musical box that plays the Brahms 'Lullaby' but your wailing
drowned out the tune. I stayed with you, stroking your wet
cheeks with my trembling fingers until eventually you slept
from exhaustion, your downy golden curls wet from my
tears and yours. Hugh was exhausted by your crying and so
full of doubts that I almost threw him out there and then,
but I couldn't deny that your life would be damaged by not
having your father at home. I wished that he could be
more positive though; every new mother needs reassurance
and I felt that he was being intolerably selfish and insensi-
tive to my needs when I overheard him in the bathroom.
'What have we done?' he was asking himself, over and
over again. 'Oh, what have we done?'

Hugh and I went to bed straight after the nine o'clock
news. He was so agitated by then and I didn't want to be
too tired when you woke up early. Hugh took a sleeping
pill but I lay awake, tiptoeing out to you every now and
then to watch you sleep in your cot. You must have had a
nightmare at about one in the morning because you started

to scream. I went into your room and you were lying on your back, eyes wide with terror, fists clenched above the blankets. I took you out of the cot and into my bed, where you would not be comforted. Your body was a rigid arch and your head thrown back. I stroked you and sang to you and eventually you relaxed and took the bottle of warm milk. You suckled it dry and then curled into me like a bear cub.

In the morning, Hugh brought in some clean clothes for you to wear: some tiny blue and white striped velvet dungarees and a navy-blue cardigan that his mother had knitted. I fingered the clothes but could not bring myself to dress you in them, for they were the clothes of the other child. Hugh seemed cross, but at least after his night's sleep he appeared to have become a bit more sensitive to a new mother's needs and we didn't have the customary huge row. Instead, I sent him out to Baby Gap in Oxford Street to buy you some new clothes all of your own. You look beautiful in plain white, so I asked him to get some white Babygros too, from Marks and Spencer's, who make them from the softest towelling. I can't abide all those baby clothes that are made from stiff fabrics with itchy labels and bulky seams, so irritating to a tender young skin – they may be all right for other people's babies but not for mine, thank you very much.

I was quite pleased when he was gone and switched the heating up full. I ran a bath of warm water and we splashed together and played with the tiny sailing boat that I had been saving for you. You gurgled with pleasure as I

filled my mouth with bathwater and spouted out a stream
like a whale, and then you gurgled some more as I sang
'I'm Forever Blowing Bubbles' with my mouth under the
water. I wrapped us both in a large towel and put *The
Carnival of the Animals* on the gramophone, and then I
waltzed with you around the flat, deliciously nude with my
new baby, skin to skin.

I don't think a new mother has ever been happier
than I was while we were together. I know that other
people are surprised by how much time a baby takes up. I
hear them complain that they no longer have even a
moment to read the newspaper. The very idea of reading a
newspaper when there is a tiny person who needs attention! I have always found it quite puzzling that anyone
with a new baby should want to do anything other than
delight in something as amazing as that baby. There wasn't
a moment that I was with you that I didn't thank my lucky
stars. There wasn't a moment that I wanted to do anything
other than hold you or sing to you or even just watch you
as you slept. I marvelled at your perfection, at the curling of
your new hair at the tender nape of the neck that I had to
kiss each time I saw it, at the way your tears made your
lashes into the points of a star around the concentrated
cobalt of your eyes. Sometimes I would have to remove
one of your socks just so I could hold the smooth perfection of a chubby pink foot and kiss the tiny toes.

I knew it would be like this from the first moment I
saw you. I loved you with a mother's love – fierce and protective – as soon as our eyes met. You held your arms out

to me while *that other woman* was stacking her trolley from the Ready Meals freezer at Nu-Save. You were propped in the front of her trolley, without a harness to keep you safe, too young to be made to sit in the wire and plastic trolley seat all unsupported like that. There was another child with you, aged about four, a girl with a snotty nose and golden studs in her ears. She was whining and holding on to that woman's fuzzy grey coat. The woman was cross with the little girl and kept telling her to 'Belt up before I smack you one,' or words to that effect. I felt so scared for you as I watched across the aisle, pretending to choose tinned soup. I followed you closely as that woman and the whining child wheeled you and the trolley through the supermarket. I stood quite close when she came to a stop at the BabyCare section and watched with horror as she put all manner of ready-prepared baby meals into the trolley, along with a pack of two dummies, some syrup drink of the sort that everyone knows rots new little teeth, a large drum of Cow & Gate formula and an economy packet of Nu-Save SupaSaver Nappies. You were whimpering now, obviously hungry and uncomfortable, and I nearly rescued you on the spot when the woman said, 'And you can shut up an' all.'

Hurriedly I added some of the ghastly baby meals, the tooth-rotting syrup, a tin of formula and a packet of two dummies to my basket. Obviously I didn't want you to be too upset when you first came to me and I thought it would be easier if you had what was familiar at first. I would soon get you on to a healthier diet, I knew. If you

needed dummies to soothe you at first, then so be it. I drew
the line at the cheap nappies, though. I just couldn't bear
the thought of your getting sore and so I put a small packet
of Pampers into my basket. I stood behind you at the
checkout. The woman found that one of her cartons of
milk was leaking and left you sitting there while she dashed
off to change it, with the little girl still trailing at her side.
There you were, whimpering and alone; quite honestly,
anyone could have taken you.

When she returned with a new carton of milk, the
little girl wanted some of the sweets that were displayed
there along with the women's magazines. She wailed as
that woman finally did smack her, hard, on the back of the
legs. You were crying too by now and our eyes met once
again. Silently, I promised you that I would save you.

The woman was packing her trolleyload into bags as
I paid for my modest basket of goods. I trailed you out to
the car park and threw my carrier bag and sheepskin jacket
into the boot of my car while I watched the woman load-
ing up her Vauxhall with the shopping, the little girl and
you, making my blood boil by dumping you like a bag of
laundry into your car seat, banging your head as she did so.
I moved my car to the exit, dropped the relevant coins
into the machine and got through the barrier. I parked
just down the ramp and waited. Then I followed the
Vauxhall through the rush-hour streets as it headed west. I
even had to jump a red light to keep up but I wasn't prepared to lose you for anything by now. I thanked God that
I had been prepared for this day and your beautiful cot was

finished and ready at home. If it had been two weeks earlier the paint would still have been wet and that wouldn't have done at all.

God was on my side that day. The Vauxhall stopped at the corner of the old high street, right outside the off-licence, and the woman got out. She didn't even have the grace to look guilty as she headed in, leaving you and the other child unattended in the car. As I pulled up in front of the Vauxhall, the small girl got out of her seat and followed her, leaving you alone in your car seat. I knew it was meant to be then and I pounced, sure that what I was doing was the right thing. I opened the car door, swiftly undid your seat harness and ran with you back to my car. Oh my love, how I wish it could have been a gentler journey but I could see no other way in my haste to rescue you. I had to bundle you into the boot of my car, thankful for the sheepskin jacket that was stowed there, and take off for home. The whole thing took no longer than a minute. My hands were shaking, of course, as I steered the car and I had to keep telling myself that this new journey was no worse than birth, what with all that bumping and squeezing. When I got back, I put the car into the garage before opening the boot, and there you were, none the worse for the journey, screaming with the vigour of the newly born.

I have nothing to say to my interrogators as we sit in my sitting room. They want to know where Hugh is but I say that he walked out some time in the summer. The social worker has gone into your nursery, and I hear you scream as she picks you up, waking you from your sleep. The policewoman puts my hands behind my back and into handcuffs and I am led outside into the snow. As they unlock the police car I twist my right hand up and cut my left wrist, straight across the radial artery, just as I planned, with the razor blade that I had kept on the hall table ready for this day. At the same time the social worker comes out with you wrapped in a blanket. You are screaming as you pass me and I turn my body round to shield you from the drops of blood that are spilling from my wrist. I don't want you to remember me like this. I don't want you to see my blood roses in the snow.

Turkish   Carpets

Their plane has been delayed. They discover this when they arrive at Dalaman Airport. Robert checks his watch. 'Right, two hours,' he says and swings the little girl back on to his shoulders and ushers the two women back outside, to the hairdryer heat and the waiting taxi.

He sits in the back with Florence on his knee. 'Here, my arms are your seat-belt,' he says, linking his fingers around the squirming child's tummy.

Leoni, the girl's mother, sits next to him on the hand-covered orange velour seat, strokes Florence's fringe out of her eyes. Robert's wife, Clara, takes the front seat, staring ahead at the miniature plastic mosque that is perched on top of the dashboard and at the string of amber-coloured worry beads that hang from the rear-view mirror. The driver, silent, resentful, fits an implausible amount of luggage into the boot of the old brown Chrysler, humping suitcases, travel cot, pushchair and carpets, and finally accepts defeat and, glaring at Clara, opens her door. 'You will have to take these in the front with you,' he mutters, pushing the two rolled-up carpets into the space at her feet and over her legs.

'We have two hours,' says Robert. 'Will you take us somewhere local with good food?'

'Tamam,' says the driver. 'OK.'

'Perhaps you could take us to *your* favourite restaurant in the town,' says Clara. Her mind is already home. She is thinking of her Persian cats. They will be pleased to see her.

They drive from the airport, the roadside sprouting dusty oleanders. The radio wails with the calls of the mosque, the little girl fiddles with the buttons on Robert's shirt. 'Open seat-belt,' she says. 'Oh no,' says Robert, tickling her beneath the ribs with his thumbs.

Clara folds her hands around the carpets, links her fingers. There. She is a seat-belt too. The carpets feel rough and knotty beneath her hands. Clara and Robert like to buy something for their house wherever they travel. And they travel as much as they can. At home, they sleep beneath an inky-blue batik bedspread from their honeymoon in Bali. They eat their cereal from Andalusian cream and blue earthenware bowls and play Perudo at their coffee table from Rajasthan, a large carved rosewood affair with big iron rings at each corner that was once a ceremonial marriage bed. They keep their fruit in a glowing bamboo lacquered bowl that Clara spotted in a Vietnamese market.

This year Robert wanted a Turkish carpet, not just any old rug but a proper antique. This year Clara wanted a baby. Last year Clara wanted a baby too (Robert decided to buy her an uncut emerald to celebrate their fifteenth year together, so they went to Colombia instead). The year before that Clara wanted a baby too. That year they went to China and as a result a carved jade Buddha graces the mantelpiece in their drawing room. 'Quite a find, that,' says Robert.

Robert and Clara work for an overseas aid organisation. He knows much about global overpopulation, antique textiles, tribal art and birth control. And so does Clara.

'I know, I know,' she says, twisting the emerald ring around her finger as the conversation takes its path, predictable as noughts and crosses. 'There are too many children already.'

'Only an egomaniac needs to reproduce his own image,' he tells her, the words familiar as a mantra. 'If I need to see myself, I have only to look in the mirror.' And what a mirror: French, Louis XIV, ornately framed antique mercury glass with the diffuse sparkle unique to old glass, found by Robert in Champagnac de Belair. Now it reflects their every movement as they argue on the bed.

'And I like things the way they are, just the two of us,' he says. 'If we had children we wouldn't be free to travel like we do. We wouldn't be able to afford it, for one thing.' Clara thumps the pillow, wishes she didn't love him.

He suffers by being right. Clara knows him well enough. Besides, what is the alternative? Robert is the only man she truly likes. He is kind and he is handsome as a lion. She watches her friends marry men she cannot imagine waking next to and feeling anything but despair. Bores and drunkards. She watches her friends divorce. She listens sympathetically to stories of wrangles over money and property. Such bad fathers.

'Children? No, none. But we have holidays!'

And Robert has a child. Three years ago, the day after his fortieth birthday, he 'adopted' a Sudanese orphan. A few pounds each week pays for vaccination, education and sustenance. At the office, Robert has a framed picture on his desk of a beautiful boy with wide puppy eyes.

Robert and Clara sit back to back, still fully dressed, at opposite sides of their big bed, beneath a pair of roughly carved cherubs from Mexico. Clara rests her head against the headboard, cries, silently, as she always does.

'Clara,' says Robert, 'you know how much I love children. But I'm not like you. I don't need my own. I love *all* children.'

Clara wishes that she hadn't changed. In the cold light thrown by global economics she agrees with him, but her heart keeps breaking.

'Oh Robert,' she says, 'I can't help it.'

Robert moves behind her and rubs her hunched shoulders. He often feels like crying too. 'I'm so sorry, love,' he says. 'I can't help it either. I just can't bring another person into the world. I wish I could for your sake, but I would be going against everything I believe.'

'I should leave you,' says Clara. She knows, Robert

knows, that she won't. Given the choice of Robert or a child that she doesn't yet know, he wins every time. Robert stands up. Clara turns her head, absently smooths the bed where he has been kneeling behind her.

'Look at poor Leoni,' he says to her reflection in the mirror, 'stuck at home with a baby. She hasn't been anywhere since she had Florence. You told me she was desperate for a holiday.'

'Leoni hasn't got a husband,' says Clara. 'It's not the same thing.'

Sometimes Clara thinks her friend Leoni did the right thing when, with no suitable partner in sight, she simply 'stole' a baby from some man or other. Clara has given up expecting Leoni to tell her who the father is. She suspects that Leoni doesn't know herself. Clara thinks about sweet little Florence, the way the little girl says her name, 'Cwara', and how her smile has changed now that she has cut her teeth, the way her hand feels like a tiny warm paw.

'Robert,' she says, 'do you think we could treat Leoni and Florence to a little holiday this year?'

Robert read a book before they came to Turkey about buying antique rugs. Not for him the machine-made kelim or factory knots of modern carpets. He had enjoyed the holiday so far: the trips they took to the roadside tombs at Daedala and the ruined city at Xanthos, and to the temples of Artemis and Apollo at Letoum, where the three of them sat atop ancient amphitheatres each night at sunset, taking turns to sing or act out monologues from the three-thousand-year-old stages below. And much as he liked the

tourist shops of Kas and building castles with little Florence
from the butterscotch sand at Patara, he was secretly impatient to get to the main business of the trip. He knew what
he wanted. Nomadic carpets, made before the turn of the
century, before synthetic dyes were imported from
Germany.

'We're going on a magic carpet hunt,' he told
Florence, as he tucked her up in the double bed that she
shared with her mother, who was standing at the door
with Clara.

'See, what a waste, he would make a great father,'
Clara whispered to her friend.

'What we need to look for,' he instructed Clara and
Leoni as they sat on the hotel balcony above the sea, 'is
imperfection.' Leoni nudged Clara, Clara raised her eyebrows and lit a cigarette. They both knew Robert well
enough to feel a long lecture coming up, and he *was*
excited about the trip to the carpet shop.

'The colours shouldn't be too uniform in a tribal rug.
Diversity of tint is one sign of a genuine antique, because,
you see, the nomads could only carry small pots for dyeing
their wool. They were unlikely to hit the same colour
twice when they made up dye baths from olive leaves,
pomegranate, saffron, walnuts, acorns, madder root and
the cochineal beetle, or rather,' he said, putting an arm
around each of the women at his side, 'the *female* cochineal,
yet another thing that only the girls of the species can do.
God, us males, bloody useless at everything.'

'Except war and long-distance running,' said Clara.

'Farting and playing electric guitar,' said Leoni.

'Being sperm donors,' said Clara, and then wished she hadn't.

'Of course,' he added, getting back to his carpets, 'there is a deliberate mistake in every rug anyway. You see, for Moslems, only Allah can be perfect.'

And with that, they went to bed, Leoni to curl herself around her sleeping child and Robert and Clara to make quiet, careful and considerate love, a pillow wedged between the headboard and the wall to stop it banging, anxious as parents not to wake the little girl in the next room.

'Look at the knots,' he said, just before they fell asleep. 'We should not consider anything with fewer than three hundred knots to the inch, according to my book.'

When they got up for breakfast, Leoni was cracking open pistachios and using the fresh green kernels to write Florence's name on the table, but Florence was eating the nuts and laughing. 'Ooh, you little chipmunk,' said Leoni, play-pinching her cheeks, which sent the little girl into paroxysms of naughty giggles.

'Did you know,' she said to Robert and Clara, over Florence's fair head, 'that Gauguin told his students that if they wanted to know about technique they had only to study Turkish carpets, and there they would find all knowledge?'

Hell, thought Clara, she's been reading up, bloody show-off.

'Yes, of course,' said Robert. 'Gauguin's colours, now that's what I would like to see in my carpet.'

They took a long, hot taxi ride, along dirt tracks, above the coastal road. They swerved to avoid a large tortoise as they passed through villages of tomato houses, their aluminium frames covered in misted polythene. The polythene was ripped into ribbons in places and they could see the heavily fruiting tangled vines inside.

There were three carpet shops along the quayside in Bokarum. In each of the shops, their dazzled eyes rested on carpets hanging from the whitewashed walls, looped like hammocks from beams in the ceiling, rugs piled high in every corner in a kaleidoscope of wool and silk and camel hair. In each shop they were greeted like long-lost friends and offered tiny glasses of ata chai, served on round, engraved silver trays and made from fresh sage leaves which were still steeping in the amber tea, and for Florence there was thick, sweet fruit juice.

With a click of their fingers, the proprietors had men turning the carpets, some stacked four feet high; dark, muscular men, one at each corner, turning layer upon layer of brilliant carpets, like pages from some huge illuminated book. Each time a carpet was thumped down, streams of dust particles danced in a shaft of light from the window. 'Tamam?' asked the carpet sellers as each new rug was laid on top of its predecessor. 'You like this? Very good carpet.' But each time Robert shook his head. 'They are not old,' he whispered to Clara. 'They are not natural dyes.'

'And this one,' said Kemal, the proprietor in the third shop, 'is a very good Yuruk, from eastern Anatolia.' Kemal ran his fingers around the liver-coloured border with its geometric pattern of saffron and indigo motifs. 'The ram's horn,' he said, looking Robert in the eye, 'for masculine power and fertility, for large happy family.'

They wouldn't be taking that one then, Clara thought bitterly, as she recognised the throbbing of her womb, preparing her for this month's disappointment. Her legs and her back ached too and the air was heavy with the tang of sweat and dust from the men turning the heavy carpets. She sat down on a pile of rugs and felt like the most colourless, least alive thing in the place.

Leoni was still looking at the carpets and Florence was singing happily to herself and playing with a string of glass beads that Robert had bought her from one of the tourist shops. Clara tried to concentrate on the religious fetishism that could be found woven in the carpets; there were amulets and talismans, suns and moons and dragons, birds to mediate between the dead and the living, ewers and vases to symbolise purity and stylised combs for cleanliness. Kemal showed them what he assured them were genuine antique Tekke rugs and Salor rugs and Saryks and Gotshanak, but still Robert shook his head.

Eventually Kemal stepped back and rubbed his two forefingers together, knuckles upwards, like a cricket rasping its legs. 'Argadesh, argadesh,' he said to Robert. 'We are brothers.' He could see that he would not make a sale from the tourist carpets. They had reached the end of the third pile and he clicked his fingers for more tea. He stroked Florence's hair. 'So pretty,' he said, and then to Robert, 'You will not buy these carpets. I take you to very old carpets.

Very old. Very good. My father's shop in Kekova. We take a boat there, tomorrow. Yes?'

'Argadesh,' said Robert, rubbing his own forefingers together, beaming, and they arranged to meet at the quay the following morning.

Clara was still weary the next morning, her head heavy as a watermelon on the hotel pillow. 'I don't think I'll be good company today,' she told Robert, who almost forgot to be sympathetic such was his excitement about the carpets. 'My period pains and this heat. I think I'll stay here and read my book.'

'Hi,' said Leoni, bringing her orange juice in one hand, Robert's guide to buying tribal rugs in the other, and dressed in khaki linen and white pumps. 'How do I look? Would you sell your family carpet to this woman?' The holiday had done her good, smoothed her face. Florence ran in behind her, in a dear little broderie anglaise dress, and jumped up and down on the bed.

'You poor old thing, there's really nothing worse in this heat, is there?' Leoni said, catching Florence before she fell.

It was the pain in her head more than menstrual cramps. The handy once-monthly letter to the games mistress of her girlhood ('Please would you excuse Clara from gym this week . . .'), the relief each month of her teenage years ('Thank you, God!'), that in Clara's case extended into the first ten years of married life, were now replaced by a vacuous sorrow. A nebulous grief for someone who didn't exist. A few more years and this monthly reminder would cease. She felt that she was becoming extinct.

'You're getting depressed again, aren't you?' said Leoni, pulling back the curtains so that Clara could see the hazy blue sea meet the sky.

'I just feel so sad, stupid really,' said Clara. 'There doesn't seem to be a solution. I look at people, married people with children, and, well . . . Have you noticed how much they start resenting each other as soon as they have children?'

'Time and again,' said Leoni. 'You and Robert are about the only couple I know who are actually quite nice to each other.'

Leoni stopped telling Clara the truth soon after Florence was born. She emphasised the bad things about her new motherhood: the sleepless nights, the tantrums, the men who wouldn't come near. She daren't mention how her veins were filled with a new warmth, how everything in the universe had taken on a new significance now that she had Florence. She told Clara how much she envied her her freedom, her social life, her taut stomach muscles and her elegant home that didn't house even an ounce of Fisher Price primary-coloured plastic. Sometimes Clara even believed what she said.

'God, the extra burden,' Leoni told her friend, 'of a night out. Leaving Florence with a babysitter, she always cries, and the expense! It means that there is always such an onus on the quality of an evening. One long dull joke, and I'm looking at my watch, calculating the cost before the punchline.'

But despite her friend's efforts, nothing could shift

Clara's self-pity by the time they had to leave for the carpet shop. Leoni and Florence accompanied Robert on the boat ('No, no, of course you must go, it will be lovely for Florence to go on a boat, I'll be fine after today, I'm sure') and Clara stayed behind at the hotel, read her book, smoked too many cigarettes and took a stroll down to the harbour to buy some more.

It was quite late when she heard voices coming up the street. She went to the balcony and there she could see her husband, her friend and the little girl walking up the path. Robert and Leoni were swinging Florence between them. The sun was behind them, setting, their hair three blazing halos. As they got closer, Clara suddenly thought with a jolt how like a perfect family they looked.

Two large men followed them, a pair of carpets rolled over their shoulders. Robert has bought one for Leoni too. How kind he is! He spread it out beneath the balcony where Clara sat smoking and did an imaginary magic carpet routine with the little girl. He kissed her while she rode through the cloudless sky on the crest of a flying carpet of many colours. Look at Robert. He loves children. He loves *all* children. The holiday was at an end. His mission accomplished.

The luggage forms a rude pile on the pavement outside the café. Clara's big brown suitcase, Robert's smaller matching suitcase and folding suit-carrier, Leoni's three squashy coral-coloured holdalls with thick leather straps, the travel cot in its neat navy-blue carrier, the child's little powder-blue pigskin suitcase, and on top of it all, the two carpets, rolled inside out, forming a swath of aubergine, saffron, indigo, cadmium and viridian.

'How these will brighten all our lives!' says Leoni, eyeing the beautiful carpets, as she snaps the pushchair together and Robert lifts her daughter into the seat. Clara rummages in Leoni's worn purple velvet travel bag and finds Florence's sunhat. The café is open to the street, just half a dozen long tables covered with white paper. The sun streams down through a rough canopy of rafters and bamboo sticks. The pavement café is between two building sites. The traffic roars past on the road to the airport.

'Bring us some plates of your specialities,' says Robert with mock grandeur to the sleepy man behind the smeared glass food display.

A small boy picks his way through the rubble of scaffolding made from bark-covered saplings nailed with a latticework of poles on the neighbouring building site. He is thin, in a grubby turquoise T-shirt and bagging tracksuit bottoms that are worn through at both knees. He is carrying man-size rubber flip-flops and a plastic carrier bag. As he approaches, they see that his hands are black.

Robert is wrestling with Florence's pushchair, trying to manoeuvre it between the tables. The boy takes the other side of the pushchair, gesturing with his filthy hands that he will help to lift it over the obstructing table. Robert waves him away – almost, Clara thinks, shoos him away. The boy steps back as his friend, older and thinner, with a tragic lopsided face, joins him at the café. He might be smiling, but with his disfigured face it looks as though he is leering through his gash of a mouth.

The two boys move away and squat in the dirt a couple of yards from where Robert has now lodged the pushchair between the tables. Robert picks up Leoni's velvet bag and his camera case and moves them closer, and winds the handles around his chair leg.

Clara feels so sad as she looks from Florence, fussing over her chips, wanting ketchup, to the two boys, dejected and ragged, on the building site. The boy in the turquoise T-shirt has cut his foot on a rusty nail. He sees Clara looking at him. 'Hey, miss.' He shows her his foot.

'Ignore them,' hisses Robert. Clara turns her face back to the food. Flies buzz around the meat. She doesn't feel hungry. Leoni has Florence on her lap. Robert is playing aeroplanes with the chips.

Clara reaches in her bag for her cigarettes. She takes one from the packet but her lighter has stopped working. The boy is at her side. 'Here, miss.' He hands her a flattened box of matches, warm, from his tracksuit pocket.

'Thank you,' says Clara, lighting her cigarette. The boy smiles. Remains at her side.

'Oh for God's sake,' says Robert, 'just give him something and tell him to go away. We haven't got time for all this.'

'Here,' says Leoni, producing a colouring book and some crayons from her velvet bag and sliding them over the table to Clara. 'Florence won't miss these.'

Clara smiles back at the boy and gives him the book

and crayons. He takes them quickly, as though he thinks she may change her mind. 'I don't think we've seen the back of them,' says Robert.

'They're only children,' says Clara.

'Rather unhygienic children though,' says Leoni. 'Poor things.'

Robert is the only one who is eating. The flies on the food don't bother him. 'Perhaps you shouldn't let Florence eat any of the meat,' he says, between mouthfuls.

The two boys are back. The older boy points at Robert's shoes. 'Oh God, he wants my shoes now,' says Robert. 'No, no. Go away.'

The boy keeps pointing. 'I said no,' says Robert. 'Now, away.' He waves his napkin at the boys, disturbing the flies. The boys step back. Their hands really are filthy.

The boys sit in the dirt, absorbed now, colouring pictures from the book. The smaller boy looks back at Clara and holds up his work for her to see. He has coloured a tiger in red and yellow stripes, surrounded it with purple and orange flowers. He is smiling now, waiting for her approval. Clara gives him a thumbs-up sign, smiles back. His friend has carefully taken a page from the book and holds up his picture of a seal balancing a ball on its nose for her to see. More thumbs up. Leoni claps her hands.

Leoni hugs Florence closer to her chest. She is crying. 'That's my book,' she wails.

'When we get back to England, do you know what I'm going to do?' Robert says. 'I'm going to buy you the biggest colouring book in the shop.'

Clara watches the two boys as they wander past the café, showing their pictures to passers-by. The bigger boy slaps his on to his forehead and struts. Clara imagines smuggling one of the boys to England wrapped in a carpet like Cleopatra, and Robert's face when he unrolls the carpet in their lovely eau-de-Nil drawing room and a small Turkish urchin spirals out at his feet. She silently conjures a picture of herself singing lullabies to a sleepy dark child in the little room that she secretly thinks of as 'the nursery'. The two boys walk past the café again. Florence has stopped crying. The smaller boy points at the colouring book and the crayons and then to himself, a question.

'Yes, for you,' Clara gestures back. He points again at Robert's shoes. 'No, no, just the crayons,' she says. He smiles, gives her a thumbs-up, opens his plastic carrier bag. It holds a blackened duster, some brushes and shoe polish, brown and black. He puts the crayons inside and, still smiling, backs out of the restaurant.

Subterfuge

What sort of job is this? I stand in the department store, dazzling in my white coat, spraying people as they go by with Passion or L'Air du Temps. 'Do you mind?' some say, while others cough dramatically into their husband's handkerchiefs as they go by. Sometimes I think of it as target practice: I take aim at women shoppers who dare to circumnavigate me in that exaggerated, self-important way they have.

It was never intended that I should work in a shop, of course. Back in the days when my wickedness simply served as a sign of my great intelligence, I was told, 'You'll end up behind the counter in Woolies,' whenever I was late with homework or caught skiving; drinking Coca-Cola in the bus station café with my collar turned up as protection from the prying eyes of passing teachers. But my mother knew that I was destined for greater things: 'Ooh, she is an 'orrible little girl,' she would say, but her eyes were bright and her smile indulgent. It was ''orrible' with the aitch dropped in affection. It was ''orrible' in the way that a cream cake is 'naughty'. Naughty but nice, that is.

Back in the days when I was cherished as a clever child with a wicked sense of humour, my parents gave me one of those children's play shops, complete with miniature cardboard packets of cornflakes and Daz, thimble-sized tins of baked beans and Jolly Green Giant corn, plastic loaves of bread and tin money that went into a little till that rang in a convincing way whenever it was opened.

I was forever adding to the provisions in my shop with plasticine fruit and slices off the bath soap for cheese. None of this interested Patrick, my brother, who at eleven years old would not be cajoled into playing the customer. At least that *was* the case, until the day he noticed what was serving as a bottle of wine on the shelves of my store: our babysitter had given me an empty miniature green glass Brut aftershave bottle.

As no one else would play, I was forced to kidnap Wilbur, Patrick's beloved guinea pig, from his hutch and was attempting to train him to play the part of busy house-wife by adding scoops of guinea pig food muesli to the wares on special offer in my bedroom. Patrick, furious as ever, came storming in to rescue his pet, snatching him from the counter and knocking over my entire display stand. I started a theatrical wail and, terrified of recrimination, he resigned himself to helping me restack the shelves.

Suddenly his eyes alighted on the once empty, now filled with water, Brut bottle.

'You don't want this,' he said, snatching the bottle.

'Yes I do,' I replied, snatching it back. 'It's white wine.'

Patrick, momentarily forgetting Wilbur, went to his own room and returned with a sixpence and a soft smile.

'I'll give you this for the wine,' he offered, lovingly.

'Can't you read, sir?' I replied in my best grocer's voice. 'That wine costs two shillings.'

Common sense departed in Patrick's lust for such a manly accoutrement. Always a sucker for advertising, he handed over the full asking price.

The bottle was too small for him to be able to 'splash it on all over' as Henry Cooper had instructed on the telly, but the sight of poor Patrick dabbing on slightly perfumed water moved my father (once he, my mother and I had all had a surreptitious snigger) into swapping the dud for a real bottle of the sickly scent. My white wine was returned to the shop and I got to keep the two shillings too. Retailing seemed to me a jolly good trade to be in, back then.

'Oh, you 'orrible, 'orrible little girl,' said my mother, tickling me until I squealed. You see, when I was young, I could wear my naughtiness like a tarnished halo. Patrick never quite managed my brand of 'orrible; he simply didn't have my spirit. At least, that's what I heard my mother telling my father, on one of the many occasions that I eavesdropped, late at night, at their bedroom door.

I remember the time, when Patrick was at college and I was still at school, that he came to me for advice.

Unlike my blissfully unsuspecting parents, he knew that I had long since graduated from snogging competitions behind the drama hut at lunchtimes to a full social whirl of youth centre discos and the serial relationships that went with them (a sort of pubescent version of wife-swapping, I suppose). I plucked my eyebrows to a line of single hairs and wore crucifix earrings. On my middle finger I twisted my boyfriend's eight-piece puzzle ring, and beneath my collar were hidden the mulberry bruises of his love bites.

By the time I had that steady boyfriend with an ear-ring, a nickname, a motorbike and a police record, Patrick was still unsnogged and something of an embarrassment to me, in his straight-leg cords and Harris tweeds. I wished I could trade him in for a brother who looked more like Marc Bolan, the sort of brother my friends might fancy. I supposed it was because I knew about the importance of Falmer flares and Dolcis platforms that he thought I was qualified to advise him in the matter of Julie Harvester.

I could always tell when he had something on his mind. He seemed nervous making his cup of Nescaff and I sat and waited, drumming my heels on the Aga, cramming toasted Marmite sandwiches into my mouth.

'You'll get piles if you sit there,' said my mother, passing through.

'Piles of what?' I replied, imagining gold bars stacked up like a hay rick.

She shot me her look, her secretly amused 'Oh, you are 'orrible but I love you anyway' look. At least that's what I took it to mean when she narrowed her eyes and pursed her drawstring lips like that.

Patrick added my Radio One Roadshow mug to the tray he had been planning to take up to his room, where, unasked by Tolkien, he was laboriously illustrating *The Lord of the Rings* in cross-hatched biro, filling six sketchbooks and three of my school jotters.

'That's my mug,' I growled, irritated that he always took it and left it to grow penicillin in the purple pit that served as his bedroom. He shot me a look of sibling hatred, removed the cup and then looked again, smiled and cleared his throat.

'What do you think about a girl asking a boy out?' There, he'd said it, all in a rush.

'Depends what she's like,' I said, carefully peeling a couple of split ends I had noticed, lit like fibre optics, against the low light of the west window, wondering if perhaps he was gay.

'She seems OK,' he said, reddening at the temples. 'She's doing a secretarial course at the tech.'

'And she's asked you out? Is that what you're saying?'

Patrick, always awkward in his six-foot-three frame, suddenly looked comically much too large for the tiny cottage kitchen as he concentrated extra hard on stirring his four sugars into his coffee.

'Yes. No. Not exactly. But her friend told me she fancies me and that she *wants* to go out with me.'

'I see,' I said. 'Well, you have to decide if you think she's a slag. Maybe she is and that's why she asks boys to go out with her. But if she's not a slag, then I suppose it's OK.'

I had a simple view in these matters. Quite what qualified a girl as a 'slag' I wasn't sure. I just knew I wasn't one. The girl who had gone out with my boyfriend before me, now *she* was a slag. She had shagged him behind the community centre on their first date. I didn't think Patrick should go out with someone like that.

'She's quite pretty, I think. About sixteen. Lives in Summercombe. She's called Julie. I've never seen her with any boys though.' Patrick obviously didn't have a clue.

'Yes, yes,' I said, impatient now, 'but what does she wear?' I thought that if he could at least describe how she dressed I would be able to tell him whether he should get to know her better or not. 'Oh, and does she use loads of make-up, you know, like too much black eyeliner?'

'Eyeliner . . . er. No. Dresses. Yes, she wears dresses. And blouses.'

He looked hopeful and I decided that even a girl-friend who wore blouses was better than no girlfriend at all. Besides, I couldn't wait to tell Mum the good news. Patrick was about to get his first girlfriend.

'Invite her round some time,' I said, jumping down from the Aga. 'I'll tell you what I think afterwards.'

Julie Harvester became a regular visitor to our house where, I seem to remember, she did a lot of washing-up.

'She's very good for Patrick,' my mother said when-ever I tried to draw attention to Julie's pedestrian attitudes.

'And I do wish you wouldn't go out wearing all that black nail varnish, it makes you look so tarty.'

Whatever my mother's eyes told her, she believed that I was still her little girl. I quite consciously allowed her to think that I was simply trying on womanhood for size, in the manner of my younger self, making her laugh, clopping around her bedroom, tiny feet lost in her best black patent court shoes. But circumstances were forcing me out into the open.

'Hannah,' whispered Julie to my mother one day when we were all sitting down to lunch, 'I think you should go to the bathroom.'

Julie was blushing. My mother looked up, puzzled, as she placed the roast potatoes on the table. I was sitting in the corner seat, jammed in between my father and Patrick, panicking.

'But why?' said my mother.

I knew why. Oh God, this was dreadful. Blast Julie Harvester. Blast that I was trapped in the corner, struggling to get up, my face on fire.

'I think you've left something in there,' replied Julie, eyes gesticulating wildly in the direction of the bathroom.

My mother left the room, still puzzled. I gasped. I ducked under the table and crawled out through a sea of legs – Father's Hush Puppies, Patrick's Dunlop Green Flashes, Julie's American Tan tights and brown leather sandals – trying to escape, as my mother shouted my name from the bathroom. In her hand was my Dutch cap. I had left it drying on the side of the bath.

'What is this?' she hissed through thin lips.

'I dunno,' I said, but I knew I wouldn't get away with it. 'It's Miriam's. She asked me to look after it,' I added, implausibly.

My mother thumped her forehead with the heel of one hand, and with the other, handed it to me, dangling it between finger and thumb like a dead mouse.

'Well, tell Miriam that I don't want it here.' She barely moved her lips as she spoke, dull eyes avoiding the lies in mine.

Later that afternoon, Julie went out and returned with a large bunch of daffodils, which she presented to my mother with a sympathetic hug. Anyone would think that it was Julie, and only Julie, who understood my mother's misery that day.

But it was to my bedroom that my mother came for solace, late in the night, just as I knew she would. I lay in my single bed with the worn silky ribbon of my baby blanket pressed to my cheek, eyes closed and listening as she prayed in the dark. 'My little girl,' she whispered, finally, standing over my sneaky, composed slumber, 'don't grow up before your time.'

I hid so much from her throughout that final year. She would wave me off, each weekday morning, neat plaits dangling down the back of my school blazer, never once seeing the platform shoes that I kept in my locker at school, unaware of how I rolled over the waistband of my navy-blue skirt and pulled the ends of my blouse into a knot below my ribcage. Her job was to launder my white cotton starter bras and navy-blue school pants, and remain unaware of the secret horde of lace and satin and under-wiring hidden at the back of my wardrobe.

My subterfuge protected her from the truth. How could she have had any idea of what would happen if she left me to my own devices that summer weekend? A fif-teen-year-old girl and her sensible older brother, alone in the house, just shouldn't have precipitated so much trouble.

'It's my homework,' I lied. 'I would come, but I've got so much revision to do.'

'I'd better stay here and keep an eye on things,' said Patrick, looking from me to my mother, studiedly knitting his eyebrows together. So concerned.

No way was our aunt's funeral an exciting enough proposition to tempt him away from the pristine delights of Julie Harvester, nor me from the musky ardour of my boyfriend.

'There's food in the fridge. Look after each other. Please go easy on the telephone,' said my mother, 'and,' she continued, momentarily excluding Patrick from her gaze and concentrating her searchlights on me, 'no funny busi-ness just because we're out of the house. I don't want that Miriam here, OK?'

'Miriam, no, of course not,' I said.

The moment the brown Cortina disappeared down the drive, Patrick headed for the telephone. I hovered, shifting from foot to foot, staring at my watch, glaring. He was on the phone to Julie, giving her shorthand dictation, yes, really he was, helping her to get her speed up for her exams.

'Dear Mr Boots, Mr Shoes, our managing director, has asked me to reply to your letter of the second of February . . .' His voice droned on and on. I needed to use the phone. I had promised my boyfriend that I would call the moment the coast was clear. I was impatient for the sound of his Suzuki 250.

'Patrick,' I interrupted crossly.

'Fuck off,' he spat, covering the receiver so as not to offend the aspiring secretary.

I remained in the hallway. Mr Shoes seemed to delegate everything to his secretary, who, I ascertained from the one-sided conversation, was not allowed to stay at our house later than eleven o'clock, what with the parents being away.

It was a great night at the pub. I drank rum and black-currant and still managed to win at pool. We hid the motorbike at the end of the drive: the last thing I needed was Patrick coming on the responsible grown-up and forbidding my boyfriend from staying the night. Stifling giggles, we made it past the sitting room and to my bedroom, where I stuffed the handle of my hairbrush under the door to prevent Patrick bursting in on us. I put 'Houses of the Holy' by Led Zeppelin on repeat to drown out any telltale noises, and a red lightbulb in the anglepoise. We swigged from a bottle of Southern Comfort, pulling the eiderdown off my single bed to make a nest big enough for two on the floor.

When we awoke, sticky and stiff, I ventured out to check on Patrick. He had already left for his weekly tennis game with Julie. We brought the motorbike out from behind the hedge and parked it in front of the cottage, then cooked fried eggs and baked beans.

'Oh, you're here again,' said Julie, fresh as a daisy, still in her white tennis dress and looking at my boyfriend with the sort of warmth normally reserved for a spraying Tom cat.

'I don't suppose you'll be wanting to join Patrick and me for a game of Scrabble,' she added, adjusting the hair grips that kept her sensible bobbed hair from her eyes.

'Scrabble?' he asked. 'What's that then?'

I stood behind Julie, shaking my head and making slicing motions with my finger at my throat to show him just what I thought of her suggestion. Scrabble? No way.

'No, it's OK,' he said, winking at me, 'don't worry about us. I think we're going to listen to some music upstairs.'

'Not right now you're not,' said Patrick. 'We want some peace and quiet, not that thudding racket . . . She had some horrible record on all night.'

He glared at me. Resigned, we dumped our egg- and bean-smeared plates in the sink and headed outside.

We were rather excited, I do remember that. My boyfriend had scored some Dutch sensimillion in the pub and I was longing to try my first joint. A couple of years before, it had been cigarettes, stolen from Miriam's mother's handbag, and smoked in the old potting shed that I had commandeered as my den. My boyfriend and I headed for the wooden hut, sneaked in and bolted the door.

The joint was strong, much too powerful for a fifteen-year-old who had never smoked anything more wicked than an Embassy No 1. My head felt disengaged from the rest of my body as I woozily clambered on to the wooden bench that I had strewn with old paisley cushions and Salvation Army-type grey woollen blankets. My fingers tingled. I was semi-conscious for much of the time, as, in a fug of creosote, marijuana and damp wool, we made love in the greedy way that only the newly initiated do, slept and then made love again. And again. It was the middle of the afternoon when we finally came round. I was sore and very thirsty.

The hut had a small window with strange yellow towelling curtains decorated with grey and black swooping seagulls. The gulls danced before my eyes as I looked out of the window and towards the conservatory where hours before Patrick and Julie had been playing Scrabble just a few feet away. We had been noisy, and I felt embarrassed.

'Just stay here for a bit,' I told my boyfriend, pulling my T-shirt on over my head, 'and I'll bring you some tea.'

Julie was nowhere to be seen. Patrick was sitting alone in front of the television, not watching it, but sketching furiously.

'You're a fucking little slut,' he said when he saw me.

'And you're a lanky streak of piss,' I replied.

In a flash he was up, face white as lightning as he struck me as hard as he could on the side of the head. I was knocked to the floor. As I struggled to stand, he hit me again. With each blow I saw white flashes; my ears were ringing, my nose started to bleed. I was too shocked to feel the impact of his fists and kept trying to get to my feet. Each time I was up, he hit me back down again.

'I'll get you back, you bastard,' I screamed as, finally, I ran for the door. 'I'll fucking get you back.'

'I suppose you'll get one of your tough motorbiking friends to beat me up,' he sniggered. But he was frightened.

If I am to be honest, I did quite want my boyfriend to go on the attack when I tore back into the hut, hysterical and bleeding. But when it came down to it, he didn't feel the same way.

'What a git,' he said. 'I'd like to break his face.'

'You have my permission,' I ventured. I could taste blood in my mouth.

'I can't do that,' he said, staring daggers up at the house. 'Your parents would never let me near you again. Be sensible. You'll have to try and get over it.'

It was my boyfriend who persuaded me back into the house, cleaned me up, gave me a brandy. We lay down in my room and I cried for a long time. When we emerged, Patrick was watching *The Man From Uncle*. I started noisily making coffee.

'Make me a cup,' he shouted, his tone deliberately brutal, as though I wouldn't dare not do as he commanded from that moment forth.

My nose had started bleeding again and I went to the bathroom cupboard for more cotton wool to staunch the flow. On the top shelf, next to the rusting tin of Andrew's Liver Salts and the sticky Benylin bottle, was a large screw-top canister of Senokot, each little mossy pill capable of relieving the most stubborn constipation. I took down the canister, counted out the entire contents into my shaking hand. Eighteen pills. They took some grinding up in the pestle and mortar and I was terrified that Patrick would be able to taste them when I added the whole lot to his coffee. I put in five spoonfuls of sugar and sampled it, gingerly. It seemed fine and, trembling anew, I took the emetic mugful to him. He sipped the coffee in the affected manner of the victorious, making big, stupid, exaggerated 'ahs' after each swallow.

'So,' he said again, with another sarcastic pretend smile, 'you're going to get me back, are you?'

'Yes,' I said, and left the room.

I was frightened. My boyfriend had gone home and my parents weren't due back until midnight. I stuffed the hairbrush under my bedroom door and went to bed. Some time in the night I heard their car draw up, their muffled voices through the wall as they got ready for bed. The next thing I remember was the sudden shock of cold water, and a foul smell. Patrick was standing, electrically charged, the antique chamber pot that my mother kept in the bathroom in his hand. It was empty now. Then he was crouching and groaning at the end of my bed. My parents ran in, my father's hair on end, terrified by all the screaming. Patrick crashed back to the lavatory, howling and rolling on the floor.

'What the hell is going on?' demanded my mother.

'She's poisoned me,' moaned Patrick.

'He beat me up. He made me bleed,' I screamed back, tearing off my drenched, stinking T-shirt and retching.

My mother took me by the shoulders. I was still dripping with excrement. 'What have you done?'

'Laxatives.' I started giggling hysterically.

Patrick was off the floor and into the kitchen. He re-emerged with the knife that my mother used for the Sunday joint. A long, curved carving knife with a mock-ivory handle. I fled, naked now, for the door, running for my life with Patrick and the knife inches behind me. As Patrick lunged, my father stepped in the way and he caught him with the knife in the shoulder and then fell back to the floor. The ambulance was an age coming. It took them both away, my father for dressing to the wound, and Patrick for a stomach pump.

While I was in the bath, my mother stripped my bed, throwing the stained quilt, pillows and sheets into a bin liner. I can only think that the state of the bed sent her into a mania of revulsion, because she didn't stop there. By the time I got out of the bath my secret self was laid bare. She had found me out. The wardrobe was emptied, my clothes heaped in my father's army trunk; the contents of my desk – chewed pencils, a leaking cartridge pen and graffitied grey plastic school folders – were scattered over the clothes. Another smaller suitcase housed my books and jumpers, paperbacks and T-shirts, all willy-nilly with my underwear, a tangle of satin bras and Marks and Spencer's knickers and my – until that moment – secret black lace suspender belt, junked along with strings of glass love beads, metal chokers and gemstone rings.

The wallpaper was torn in places from the ancient Blu-Tac that had held up my Roger Dean and David Bowie posters. Even my school swimming certificates had been ripped down and lay crumpled in another bin liner, along with my records and shoes.

From the drawer under my bed she had emptied the squeezed metal twist of an old spermicide tube, my five-year lockable diary, my photograph albums and the small plastic bank bag containing the remains of the sensimillion, some giant red Rizlas and two cigarettes. These she had thrown into a cardboard box, along with Lubiloo, the rag doll that she had made me out of her old tights and wool when I started nursery school, and my ancient brown bear with the leather button eyes.

Her hair was a mess, her blue poplin nightdress stained down the front. She looked me straight in the eyes, staring hard as though seeing me properly for the first time.

'I can't take any more of this, I want you to go,' she said. 'You are a horrible, horrible girl.' And for the first time, she meant it.

Nothing Personal

The baby seat is full of broken glass again. Even after Kate has cleared away the shattered fanlight and hauled the seat out of the car and shaken it on the pavement, tiny fragments remain embedded in the grey and white striped cover, glittering like mica. Nothing has been stolen from the car, because there is nothing left to be stolen. The radio/cassette player went the first time, along with all her tapes and the few twenty-pence pieces that she kept in the ashtray for parking meters. On the second occasion, an old green canvas shoe-bag containing spare nappies and a few baby toys had been glimpsed – no doubt promising all manner of riches inside – among the detritus of blackening banana skins and empty rusk packets. But it hadn't stopped there. Although she now leaves the old Renault as empty as a showroom model, it has since been broken into five more times, this being the second in a week. They even broke the window when she left the doors unlocked. It was nothing personal.

Now she won't be able to drive to the supermarket after all. She will have to wait here until the Autoglass man turns up to replace the window. 'This street,' he will say, 'it's the schoolkids that do it, you know.' The corner shop will profit from her bad luck again. Lunch will be a pot noodle, some over-ripened bananas. Or a pork pie factory-wrapped in cellophane.

No matter. Nothing has tasted right since before the baby was born. Whatever is on the plate she will have to force herself to chew, reluctant mastication in a dry mouth. Everything she cooks, or heats up, or eats straight from the tin, turns to dry lumps which hurt when she swallows. She thinks of herself as a goose with a swollen liver, feet nailed to a board, while she forces the food from a spoon into her disobedient mouth. But she has to eat, she knows that. She has to eat to stay strong for her child.

Kate doesn't look in the mirror, but in bed at night she can touch the skeleton beneath the skin. In the dark, she thinks about the witch in 'Hansel and Gretel' being given a chicken bone instead of a plump child's finger to feel. The witch will not eat her. Not yet. In the daytime she longs to comfort her baby, to cushion his dear head against her flesh, but there is no flesh and his head bangs against her breastbone. His fingers can circle her wrist.

Her baby seems to take his cue from her. She tries sweet fruit purées and custards as the book recommends, but the plastic spoon meets closed, refusing lips. When Kate works lunchtimes in the bar, Mrs Kelly from the flat upstairs takes the baby in. Lovely, plump, Irish Mrs Kelly, who feels sorry for Kate struggling and alone with her child. 'Poor thing, she never sees a soul except for the beer-drinkers she serves in the pub,' Mrs Kelly tells her husband. 'And barely more than a child herself. I don't know what her parents can be thinking of. Kate told me that they don't even know they have a grandson. You'd think they would have contacted her after all this time, wouldn't you?'

The baby eats for Mrs Kelly. 'Ooh, he loved my lamb casserole,' she says. 'He gobbled up every little bit. Greedy boy.' Kate cannot cry in front of her baby. She did that once but his eyes found hers and he sobbed too, in panic and terror and grief. His trembling as his rock crumbled before him was too distressing to witness more than that one time.

Kate wears the same clothes every day: a thin white T-shirt, old Levi jeans which are cut-off and fraying at the knees and navy-blue espadrilles. When it is cold she puts a fading blue sweatshirt on over the T-shirt. Today is just another day, she thinks, but Mrs Kelly is having none of it when she takes the baby upstairs to be minded.

'It's not right, Kate,' she says. 'You cannot go to your own father's funeral looking like that. It's not respectful.'

The baby moves without a fuss from her arms and into Mrs Kelly's. Easy as the breeze. Too easy, thinks Kate.

Kate has never been to her parents' house. Not this house, anyway. This mock-Georgian sandstone cube is the post-Kate house. The house where she grew up was very different. It had attic rooms and damp cellars, creaking doors and draughty corridors, and a gloomy yet magical garden, where the mossy lawn was blocked of all light by ancient waxy-leaved laurels and rhododendrons. At night, there were bats and screeching birds of prey and you could just make out the lights of the town eleven miles away across the valley. There weren't any neighbours within view, and none for several miles that her parents ever spoke to. They barely spoke to Kate either, but that didn't seem odd then.

This new house, the one they moved to soon after she left them forever, has the sort of curtain-twitching neighbours that doubtless make her mother feel part of a community, and it is hard imagining her mother wishing to be part of any community. There are BMWs and Volvos parked up the drives and a Sainsbury's within walking distance.

Crunching up the gravel path now, Kate feels disoriented, like in those dreams where she arrives home from school only to find strangers living there who have never heard of her and turn her away. Only now, it is in reverse because it is the house that is strange.

A clipped pair of yew trees studded with orange berries form an archway before the front door, which is painted yellow, the yellow of poison ragwort, wasps and traffic wardens. 'Such a nice cheerful colour,' she imagines she can hear her father saying.

What a strange house to find her parents in, she

thinks. Only, of course, she will never find them both here, just her mother, who is opening the door, her face blank, as she looks her only child up and down.

'You're too thin,' are the first words mother speaks to daughter after almost two years of estrangement.

They sit in the kitchen, eyeing each other suspiciously, neither one knowing what to say. This is the bit where you tell me how much he loved me, Kate thinks, but says nothing.

'How shall I live without him?' is all her mother says, wringing her wet face in her hands. But Kate cannot comfort her. She stays where she is, sitting on the kitchen stool, dangling her legs. Serves you right, she thinks. You should have made time for other people.

Kate watches her mother blowing her nose on a damp ball of kitchen roll and feels blank. She will not tell her about the baby because she doesn't deserve to know. They drink tea, which Kate makes in unfamiliar green fluted mugs. She looks around the strange kitchen for signs, for something familiar that will connect her to the tragic woman she calls Mum, but finds nothing.

Finally they see the hearse and the funeral car arriving in the street outside. Her mother tries to take her arm as they leave the house but Kate will not yield.

'Your Uncle Connor will be there. I hope that won't be a problem for you,' says her mother as they climb into the back of the funeral car.

'You mean you believe me now?' says Kate, meeting her mother's swollen eyes.

Her mother looks away. 'I don't know what to think,' she says, stiffly. 'I've wondered since you left. But I've only had your word for it. It's your word against his and I haven't heard his. How could I? He was my poor sister's husband.'

Uncle Connor. Somehow he has got from the church to the cemetery before anyone else. Kate sees him from where she leans distanced from her sobbing mother, as they sit in the back of the black Daimler, after the readings and hymns, the prayers and the eulogies that failed to move her to anything approaching filial grief. He scurries like a lanky schoolboy on hands and knees beneath the chestnut tree that will shadow her father's grave. He is picking up conkers, examining and comparing them like a diamond dealer looking at fine stones. Finally he selects one, holds it up to the light and turns it between finger and thumb before opening his jacket and slipping it into his waistcoat pocket. It is a long-standing habit of his, this taking of something from the scene.

The shiny conker will join other sentimental keep-sakes secreted in his kitchen dresser drawer: stones from the tops of mountains and the bottom of the sea, a chunk of petrified wood from a medieval forest, a stub of tallow candle from his own confirmation, the sky-blue nylon garter of a teenage prostitute, a twisted piece of metal from the fuselage of a light aircraft that crashed on landing with him on board, a crumbling bunch of wild Greek thyme tied with a yellow ribbon. Kate's hair ribbon. Connor knows the story behind each of these things. Just as some people use photographs as prompts, it is a drawerful of his autobiography.

He fiddles with the conker in his pocket as the coffin – which like all coffins appears too small to hold a man – is lowered into the hole. The sky darkens as people step forward, some sniffing into handkerchiefs, others throwing waxy Madonna lilies, thornless roses and frilly white carnations into the grave. Kate doesn't have any flowers and her mother thrusts a long-stemmed red rose at her. 'Thank you, but I think I'd rather not,' she says, deliberately stiff and tight-lipped. A dozen people, anonymous as black crows, stand on the muddy Astroturf carpet that surrounds the grave and take one last look, deep into the ground. It starts to rain then. Large pellets of water that melt the clods of earth and send the mourners back into their cars, shaking their heads and hunching their shoulders. 'He would have liked this,' says Connor to no one in particular, pointing to the sky.

Oh yes, thinks Kate, you think you know everything about everybody. But you don't. Her father and Connor met only occasionally. She can remember them spending time together only twice, but her father, as usual, only had time for her mother, oblivious to everyone else. 'A pair of hermits,' was what Connor and Aunt Maggie called them. Just her luck to have them as parents.

Kate's father spent weeks, sometimes months, away on Foreign Office business. Kate missed him when she was little but then accepted that when he returned he had eyes only for her mother. If the three of them were standing on a precipice and he could save only one, Kate was never left in any doubt that the survivor would be her mother.

The only people they had ever stayed with were Maggie and Connor, once, at their house in Somerset; and then the terrible time, soon after Maggie died, with Connor in Greece.

The thing Kate remembers from the weekend in Somerset was visiting the woods. Of course, her father hadn't joined them, preferring to stay at the house. Rubbing her mother's sore shoulders as she sat on the carpet between his knees. Kate had begged him to take her on the adventure in the woods, but he waved her away. So she had been sent out for a walk with her uncle, along with his housekeeper's boys, about her age, eight or nine, but much more confident than she was, much noisier.

Connor had taken them into the woods. Kate remembers how she wanted him to hold her hand, to show the others that they were family, but he strode on ahead like the Pied Piper, with the boys and Kate following. He taught them how to light a fire without matches. She was sent to peel curls of bark from the birch tree near the river. Connor and the boys sat on their heels on the peaty ground, making friction sparks by spinning a twig into which he had cut a groove for the string of the bow that he fashioned from a switch of willow. They conjured a fire that day but she didn't exactly enjoy it. Her bottom got wet. Connor showed the boys how to put the fire out by peeing on it and she couldn't join in. So that's penis envy, she thought, not then, but years later.

And then there was Patmos, scene of her final alien-ation from her family. Kate remembers how the day started. Her final day, not theirs: the day they put her, screaming and crying, on to a plane back to England.

She was sitting picking the sugar off a ring doughnut. Ever since they'd arrived on the island, she had felt uneasy. It was too hot and her mosquito bites were swollen. Her mother, who knew how badly she reacted, had forgotten to pack the antihistamine. But that, in Kate's view, was the least of her crimes on this, their first and last, family holiday.

'Why can't I take a friend?' Kate had asked repeatedly before they left England for what was, in a teenage girl's mind anyway, an Easter exile at her Uncle Connor's Greek retreat, on the top of a hill, miles from anywhere save a crumbling monastery. She would be hanging around, use-less, trying to get her father's attention as usual.

'It has to be peaceful. You have plenty of revision to do anyway,' replied her mother.

'But I can't revise all day every day, can I?' she grum-bled. 'Why can't I take Cathy. At least we could revise together and I'd have someone to talk to.'

'You can always talk to us, you know,' said her mother, sighing.

'Oh yeah, great. Thanks. I will enjoy that,' replied Kate nastily. She couldn't remember ever holding their attention long enough for a conversation anyway.

'Oh for God's sake, Katie,' her mother said, 'why do you have to be so horribly self-centred. My sister has died. Your uncle is in a terrible state, as am I. I don't want to go

to bloody Patmos either but he wants us to. He needs com-
forting. Stop thinking of yourself and give us all a break.'

Kate didn't really understand why her mother was
making such a meal of Aunt Maggie's death. Yes, it was sad,
but it had been expected ever since Kate could remember.
It wasn't as if the sisters saw much of each other anyway,
and whenever Kate's mother made the trip south she
returned looking drained. 'She'll not make another year,'
she always said. 'There's no stopping it now.' Poor Maggie
had been bedridden for over a year as the cancer spread,
mapping her internal geometry, marching through her
body, depriving her first of all of the chance to have children, and by the end of that February of life itself. Maggie
had always loved Easter in Greece, which was why Connor
had asked them to join him. Her ashes were to be scattered
on Easter Day.

Kate pretended that she wasn't watching her mother
as she fed a colony of large black ants on crumbs from the
doughnut. Before her, *The Catcher in the Rye* lay face down,
still on page twenty-three, just as it had been two hours
before when she brought it out into the courtyard. From
her perch behind a baby-blue flowering plumbago she
could see her mother, joined now by her father, who was
bringing two glasses of fizzy water from the kitchen. Ice
cubes clinking. His and hers. Lovers beneath the Greek
sun, arms and legs entwined like teenagers.

'I'm thirsty,' said Kate. She picked her way, painfully
barefoot, across the black and white pebbled kuklaki courtyard to the kitchen to get herself a drink.

She was eating oily black olives from the fridge, seeing how many she could fit into her mouth, when Connor walked in from the street behind her.

'Hello, lonely girl,' he said. 'Bored again?'

Kate turned around, and he watched her frantically swallowing olives, like a snake stealing eggs.

'Nobody bloody talks to me. I might as well not exist,' she said.

'That's not true. I talk to you, don't I?' He did, sometimes. When he was not sitting, folded accordion-like and morose, beneath the lemon trees, he told Kate about the madness of grief; he even said that she helped to ease his pain.

'You're like Maggie,' he said, 'a free spirit,' and he tried to force confidences from her, offering her hand-rolled cigarettes while her parents snoozed. 'A girl like you must have lots of boyfriends. I bet you make them itch.'

Connor reached past her to the fridge for yoghurt. She stepped back as he spooned it into an earthenware dish, then trickled honey in amber spirals from a spoon held high above the bowl. He pressed the honey spoon to her lips but she shook her head.

'Too old for a honey lollipop,' he said, licking the sticky spoon himself, fixing her with his cobra's green eyes. He's completely insane, Kate decided as she edged herself along the whitewashed kitchen wall and back into the glare of the courtyard.

She stood at the foot of the sunlounger, over her

parents, still entwined, forcing her shadow to fall on them. Her father opened one eye, squinting up at her.

'What is it Kate?' he asked, as her mother's head rolled on to his shoulder and she too stared up at her daughter, surprised by the woman's body she could see there, the unwittingly outlined silhouette of shocking breasts and hips in a shapeless blue cotton dress blocking the sun.

'Dad,' said Kate, 'will you come for a walk with me? There's that tiny white chapel we saw on the track to the monastery and I thought I would sketch it.'

'What, right now?' said her father, propping himself on one elbow. 'But it's so pleasant here.'

'It's my art homework,' she said. 'I'm supposed to do some studies of buildings.'

'I'll walk with you,' said Connor, still eating his yoghurt and honey as he emerged from the kitchen. 'I like it up at the chapel. Maggie and I spent some happy times there.'

Kate's father lay down again, moving his arm to cradle his wife's head closer into his neck.

'There,' he said, 'Uncle Connor will go with you if you need company.'

'Please, Dad,' she said, giving him one final chance. His last chance to save her. 'Please help me.'

The path stretched before them, a steep incline of cocoa-dusted hot stones, loose between scrubby thyme and oregano. They didn't speak as they climbed, Connor first, clambering like a leggy mountain goat. Footsure legs of sinew and muscle beneath his khaki linen shorts, his long, tanned bare back of smooth worn leather above. Kate maintained three yards between them as she followed, furiously marching in her blue dress, stumbling among the stones, digging her nails into holes in the thin plastic bag that held her sketchbook and pencils. Succulents trawled the thirsty earth, verdant fingers seeking cracks in the baked ground. The only sounds were the occasional bleats from further up the hill, shadow-shifting sheep among boulders and the old grey olive trees.

Kate's mouth felt gritty with dust as they reached the chapel, but she refused to drink from Connor's water bottle. He poured the water into his mouth and then into his cupped hands, splashing it over his high forehead, running his wet fingers over his scalp, leaving spikes of salt-and-pepper hair sticking up like a hedgehog's prickles.

She sat sketching, with her back against the remains of a dry-stone wall, her blue dress pulled tight around her bent knees and over her feet. The chapel rose out of the terracotta earth and rocks, ten feet square, brilliantly whitewashed with a stone cross over a central dome the size of a large pudding basin. The building was dwarfed by two ancient pine trees, hung with blight, like yellowing shaving foam. Connor was inside the chapel, folding from the waist to fit through the tiny arch of a door, but she declined to look inside whilst he was still there. She wouldn't speak to him, she decided, and wondered what he would find to do while she etched angry 4B lines over the glare of white paper.

Connor was still inside when she heard the noise. A faint whimpering from behind one of the pines. And there, a puppy, weakly squirming, dusty tan and white, no bigger than a mango. Kate scooped up the crying animal and held it in the bowl of her two hands. 'Connor,' she cried, 'come here, quickly.'

Connor was beside her. The puppy's eyes were still closed but it was soft and warm in her hands. And then she looked from its hungry pink mouth to an open, black-berry-jam-coloured gash in its head and saw the waxy yellow maggots, wriggling, then falling over the backs of her hands. 'Oh,' she said, confused in her pity and disgust, the puppy pulsating like a severed heart in her grasp, 'oh yuck, please take it, Connor, please.'

She thrust the puppy at Connor and started dancing around, overcome with revulsion, trying to rid herself of the maggots, wiping her hands in the bushes and swallowing hard to stem the flow of bitter water rising in her mouth. The puppy cried, soft as a human baby, cradled in the big man's hands, and Kate could see the dried, blackened thread of umbilical cord from its poor distended stomach.

'The Greeks, they hate dogs,' said Connor. 'They put out poisoned meat for them, you know. It used to break Maggie's heart.'

'What are we going to do? Where's the nearest vet?' Kate was panicking, tears streaking her cheeks.

'Vet? Don't be stupid,' said Connor savagely. 'There's only one thing we can do. We will have to put it out of its misery. Someone has thrown it here to die.'

'I can't stand it,' said Kate.

'Whatever you could do for it, and there is nothing you can do,' said Connor, 'it won't survive.'

There was a pool of muddied water from a leaking pipe that they had passed on the track. Connor carried the puppy there, and while Kate wept with sorrow, and gratitude that he was strong enough to do it, he gently laid the small body in the puddle and held it down with a flat rock until the bubbles stopped bursting on the surface of the water. They stood by the puddle, linked by sadness. Connor for his dead wife and Kate for the puppy.

'Come back to the chapel, come and see inside,' said Connor, slipping his arm around her shoulders, and this time she did.

They passed through the wooden door, painted peeling brown, and into the cavern of black, breathing incense. Their eyes adjusted to the light. The walls were painted frescoes, egg-yolk-yellow halos above peeling faces and cloaks of slate blue and carmine. Along one side a grey horse with arching neck and jaundiced eye, its quarters covered by a flowing chalky-green cape, pawed the ground; behind it, Kate could make out a hill and the remains of a castle. In the centre was an altar box with icons that glittered in the gloom. Here were golden halos, crowns, the Madonna and child in orange and blue robes.

Connor lit one of the tapered soft brown candles at the altar, and the colours brightened around them, light reflecting off a scattering of framed tourist pictures of holy figures, trinkets stuck with sequins and coral beads, some drying white carnations, curly as cabbages, and a few coins. Offerings of bunches of aromatic herbs and a potted maid-enhair fern were heaped at the base of a blackened wooden cross, and from the centre of the dome hung three zinc incense burners, like ornate silver sugar shakers.

Connor stuck the lit candle into the sand box at the altar. Held Kate's shoulders and stared into her face.

'You look like your mother, like Maggie,' he said.

'Mum always says I look like Dad.' She hated that.

'Yes,' said Connor, 'she would.'

Kate didn't need Connor to explain that her mother resented her, but he did anyway, still holding her before him. 'You are more beautiful than her, that's part of the problem.'

Kate started to protest but he continued: 'It's not that they don't want you, you know, you must try not to think that. Maggie always said that it was just that they only wanted each other and you got in the way. She always felt so sorry for you, poor dear Kate.'

Her dusty face was still striped by her tears. He slipped the yellow ribbon from her ponytail, from where it was tied behind her neck, and watched as her hair fell forward, copper slipping over his hands. 'You have Maggie's hair,' he said, as he eased her to the ground.

Kate sat stupidly on the floor of the chapel, mesmerised, while Connor knelt before her, winding her hair around his hands. Behind him she could see the grey horse pawing the ground and the flaking castle beyond. She wanted to be held now, to be comforted, as she thought about what he had said and everyone knowing that she was surplus to her mother and father's needs, and of her Aunt Maggie pitying her that much. She thought of 'poor dear Kate' as he kissed her hair, her forehead, her eyelids and her mouth. She needed him, or anyone, to want her as he lifted her dress, as tenderly as undressing a child, making a pillow for her head out of the folded cotton and kissing her neck. She clung to him as he held her and stroked her, hypnotised by the love that he spoke. And then she was shocked back into the present by the pain as he suddenly entered her, making her cry out, 'No, no, you mustn't do that,' as she came to her senses, too late for either of them.

He was lost inside her, still holding her hair on either side of her face, pushing her to and fro across the earth floor. Her eyes were shut, willing it to be a dream, as his final cries – 'Maggie, my Maggie!' – joined her gasping sobs.

Connor wants to speak to Kate as she stands at her father's grave. She looked so small and washed-out when she arrived at the church, not at all the fleshy schoolgirl that he remembers from Greece.

'I'm so sorry, Kate,' he says, his hand on her arm.

'What about?' Her eyes meet his, flaming and black out of her rain-dampened face.

'About your father. About losing your dad.' He moves his arm up to her shoulders in an effort to hug her as she moves away, her body thin and stiff as a plank.

'Oh, that. Well, don't worry about that, Uncle Con.' She spits out the word 'uncle', her voice low. 'How can you lose something you've never had, eh?'

Connor tries to speak to Kate's mother but she turns her face the other way. Kate sees her stab a finger at his chest, before she steps back and spins angrily away from him to the other side of the grave. He leaves then. Only the widow remains by the grave. Kate thinks she looks repentant.

'Here,' she says to her mother, 'throw some mud in. It's a good thing to do.'

L u c k y

You always look like Caesar in the bath. Vast and powerful, your shoulders hugged by the enamel rolled top. They are brown and speckled like a hen's egg. I look at you from my end, water up to my chin, and wonder at you. You are the most beautiful man I have ever seen, I think, but that's not what I tell you. Instead I say, 'Let's have a game of cards.' You hesitate and I try not to look too eager, but if I were a child I would have my fingers crossed and my eyes shut. I wait for you to agree, for in my heart I know you will, despite the fact that the bath is hot as I like it: hot enough to dissolve the day, but too hot for you, steam rising, making you sweat.

You rise from the bath, your body like rain. The water level drops to below my breasts. I want to tell you to forget the cards but I don't. Instead, I hug my knees to my chest and watch you, resigned as you get the wooden tray, the crumpled playing cards and some matchsticks for keeping score. The bath is empty without you. It is too large for one person, turn-of-the-century French, standing on lion's feet and steeply sloping at both ends. I jam my thighs against the sides to keep myself from slipping underwater while you count the cards into four suits, checking that there are still thirteen of each, despite the fact that the baby used the two of diamonds as a teething aid this morning. You fit the old tray with its brass handles over the bath and lower yourself back in. I lodge my feet against your knees and we dry our hands on the flannel in preparation for the game.

I love you more than I have ever loved anyone in my life. That's what I want to say, but instead I tell you that it is your turn to be dealer. These days, I have a terror of letting you see how much I need you. Superstition makes me feel it would be foolhardy to declare my hand. Besides, it has been one of those days. Earlier, when I awoke poisoned by a dream and alone, I studied our wedding photograph. Looking at it didn't make me spit fire (as occasionally it does) nor sigh with happiness (as often it does). Instead, when I saw the picture, framed in antique silver, our faces creased and mouths roaring with laughter, I just felt an unutterable sadness.

You deal. We are playing Putrida; like all the best card games a matter of luck as much as acumen, betting with matchsticks on how many tricks we will win in each hand, moving from one card each to ten, then ten without trumps and then back down to a single card. It's not the winning of tricks that gets the points, but being correct. I am usually too keen to win points and lose sight of reality, whereas you are better at coolly assessing your hand and predicting with accuracy. We are at eight cards each on the way up and for once, I am winning. You look at your cards. 'Terrible,' you moan, 'I've had nothing but rotten hands.'

'I think I'll go for the lot,' I smugly declare, lining up eight matchsticks. Then while you waver over your unpromising cards, still muttering about your bad luck, I say: 'Well, you know how it goes: "Lucky in cards, unlucky in love." You can't have everything.' I want you to exclaim the truth of this. I want *you* to say it. I want you to throw down your cards, dump the tray overboard and take me into your arms. I want the water to slosh over the sides and the playing cards to rise and fall on the waves like little rafts as you cover me with your streaming body and tell me that I am right, that you are ferociously lucky in love. But you don't. 'I'll go for one trick then,' is what you say.

We hear the baby stir in the next room, sleepy puppy whimper. 'Oh no, don't you dare,' you hiss. 'Please don't wake up.' You have been alone with the baby today. He woke before six. How many times, I wonder, have you regretted your boast about being good in the mornings? I have always told you how disabled I feel, how it seems that the cables in my arms have been cut, my hands limp and my mind resigned to its inability to fire my useless body. So, this morning (like most mornings, in fact), when the baby called the day into action, it was you, the self-professed lark to my owl, who got up and brought him into our bed. While you gave him his bottle, I tried to make myself invisible by curling into the pillows with the sheet pulled over my head. 'Please don't let him do that, I'm *so* tired,' I moaned as the baby yanked at a handful of my hair, a snake of evidence that betrayed my presence under the sheets. Meanly, I suspected that you were watching him, amused, rather than oblivious to his urgent tugs. I emerged from the protective coverings and our baby flopped on to my face, using my chin and his wet mouth to make 'mwa mwa' sounds, like a Red Indian, and you laughed with him as I tried to be tender but all the time longed for you both to go away.

You left the curtains open and I could see the darkening sky closing in and the starkness of the distant oak. The world outside was changing fast, the birdsong ceased and I could hear the clouds rumbling. Something scratched and fluttered in the eaves as I lay on the smooth white sheets and turned my face back into the pillow. Soon after that the violence erupted. I brought my arm back until my shoulder hurt and struck you with all my might. I hit you hard on the head, I slapped your face until the palms of my hands were red and stinging, and still I went on. I pummelled your chest with my fists. Again and again I hit you. Motionless, you accepted the blows, like you always do, leaving me feeling foolish and humiliated. I could see people in the shadows, tutting their disapproval of my behaviour, feeling sorry for you. But much as I always want to, I can never stop once I have started. Then I ran sobbing from the room and threw myself on to an unmade bed. I awoke, salty-mouthed and ashamed.

Sometimes I don't have this dream for three or four months and I think everything is resolved and that my anger has at last subsided, to be replaced by mature acceptance. But this morning, there I was again, alone with my shame, left with the fading image of you slumped in a chair and the incontinence of my anger.

It was that list of yours that did it. The folded scrap of paper in the back of your address book where I should never have found it. All those girls. All those *young* girls. All those girls whose names had never been spoken but who lay indexed in blue biro, some with surnames, some in capital letters, fluttering before my eyes like butterflies over the paper. That's why I insisted we get a new bed. I imagined their juices soaked into the mattress. Late at night they haunt me still, leaving their dirty fingerprints all over you while you sleep.

I awoke again much later. You brought the drowsy baby, floppy now in his grubby Babygro, and some fizzy orange Vitamin C for me. I felt better after that. The baby sucked himself to sleep on a bottle of warm milk and I built a barricade of pillows and cushions around him as he lay, open-mouthed like a choirboy, in the middle of our big bed.

Downstairs, the Sunday newspapers lay strewn on the table. Two houseflies feasted on a plastic bowl of drying paste, the remains of the baby's breakfast. His water beaker had a congealing crust of cereal around its spout. Your spent teabags as appealing as soiled mattresses seeped into a chalky puddle of spilt baby milk by the kettle.

'Look at this, Mummy,' said our older boy, holding a block of Lego, still in his pyjamas, which, like his mouth, were stained with chocolate. 'It's a going-under-water-going-to-space-going-underground car.'

'Ouch!' I stepped on a piece of scattered Lego with my bare feet. 'I bet you haven't eaten any proper breakfast. And why aren't you dressed?' I snapped.

And then to you, 'He really shouldn't be eating chocolate for breakfast, you know.'

You sighed to the ceiling. 'The baby has been a monster this morning. He whinged when I fed him. I changed his nappy. He whinged some more. I gave him water, he whinged, I gave him milk, he whinged. He just refused to stop and now I've got a headache.'

My love, I have had the most marvellous sleep and I thank my lucky stars that I have someone like you who will let me drift, undisturbed, for a whole morning in bed. What have I done to deserve you, who so sweetly takes care of the children down here while I inhabit my childless dreams upstairs? I would love to be able to say that, I really would.

But that is not what happens. 'I think he just wants a bit of your attention,' is what I state pointedly while stacking the scattered newspapers and their litter of inserts into a tidy heap.

Vogue magazine arrived this morning with the Sunday papers. On the cover is an actress with startling sea-green eyes and parted coral lips. Her breasts are plumply spilling over a mother-of-pearl sequinned dress with spaghetti straps. I hate her. She reminds me of my mother's warning while I was still breastfeeding the baby: 'You must eat more of these,' she advised, emptying smooth, ripe avocados from a brown paper bag into the fruit bowl. 'Or they'll end up like this – you can take it from me,' she added, staring at my chest and crumpling the empty bag in her hand and then opening it to show me. I had a couple of weeks on a diet of avocado sandwiches, avocado vinaigrette, avocado and orange salad and bowls of guacamole, but soon forgot.

While I was upstairs, dressing our boy and trying to express an interest in his Lego inventions, you took the magazine and seated yourself in the overstuffed kitchen chair and started flicking through the pages.

'That's my magazine and I haven't even looked at it yet.' You can have no idea how irritated I was to find you there. 'I was just coming down to read it.' I tried to smile as I said this, but what I meant was that I couldn't bear for you to look at all those childlessly perfect models in their tiny dresses and clingy little satin tops with their bared midriffs. It frightens me. You handed over the magazine, sighing,

'God, I just want ten minutes to myself.'

'Well, excuse me,' I said spitefully. 'I just wasn't aware that reading about the wonders of new liposome-enriched face creams and the importance of Herve Leger's spring collection was so crucial to you.'

I would like to be able to tell you how jealously I guard you. It would explain so much that must puzzle you. Like my bad-tempered response to certain films, or girls in red suede hot-pants. You see, I would like to protect you from images more perfect, more alluring and more sexy than my own. And they are everywhere, these girls. They read the news and forecast the weather. Hell, these days they're even on *Blue Peter*, bouncing around with sticky-back plastic and designer cleavages. Sometimes I think I would like you to go blind.

You win the next hand and the one after that too, despite the fact that you can barely see in this light. I want the lights low as a single candle when we share the bath, and not just because the water reflects them and sends a dappling of light swirls and shadows on to the ceiling above us. I tell you the light show is more beautiful like this but I don't mention that I feel overexposed when they are bright. You squint at your cards and then at me, your eyes the same permanent inky blue as our baby's.

'Isn't it strange how luck changes depending on your state of mind?' I say.

'It's not luck, it's your perception of luck,' you say, and you are right. Sometimes, when I'm down, I feel that even the playing cards are conspiring against me.

Your face is theatrical: part Marlon Brando but with touches of a Jack Nicholson-when-young wickedness. I don't like Marlon Brando or Jack Nicholson but I find you magnificent. You don't know this because I have never told you. I could tell you now but instead I pass you the flannel and say, 'You should wipe your forehead, it's getting really sweaty,' and when you have wiped the beads from your brow, 'How many tricks do you bid? Come on, do, it's your turn.'

'We have to hurry up now, I want to finish my crossword tonight.' I am turning into my mother in more ways than one. The crossword nags at me every Sunday. I have to finish it and my ambition is to win the gold-plated fountain pen prize. It's not the pen that matters so much as being able to tell people how I got it. After all, anyone can be beautiful but it takes brains to win the Sunday crossword. I love the way you try to help me with clues although you refuse to learn the cryptic crossworder's codes ('No, no,' I say. 'Can't you see? It says "sliding around"; everyone knows that that means it's an anagram'). Another thing you don't know is how helpful you often are despite this handicap, because I never tell you when you get one right, which sometimes you do.

Earlier, while we were still shouldering my unspoken resentments and the baby was in his wheeled walker, cruising around the kitchen, destroying the contents of the cupboards like a hooligan space invader, I took over the kitchen chair with the damned crossword while you cooked. That's another thing I wonder. Do you ever regret telling me that I need never cook again? Are you shocked that I have taken you at your word all these years? I don't think I could manage my egg-fried rice now, not even if I tried. You have no idea how grateful I am that you are the one who works like a short-order chef around the clock.

There's plain spaghetti with just the right amount of cheese and cream for our son, tender baby carrots with mashed potatoes and moulied chicken breast for our baby, creamy wild mushroom risotto or tuna carpaccio with truffle oil for our friends, the full roast on Sundays, and then for me – the most finicky of the lot – steak with mushroom sauce, lemon chicken just how my mother makes it, duck breasts with fresh fruit sauces and, when all else fails, hot chocolate and walnut toast spread with my favourite Pavé D'Affinois. Do you know, I think that I would starve to death without you now.

'It says "Dental trouble, question mark. Use salt repeatedly" and it's six letters,' I said, half to myself. You stopped slicing onions and celery for your stock and looked straight ahead, thinking hard, with the twin fleshy cushions of your bottom lip sticking out like a child's, like our child's.

Our son burst into the room. 'Daddy, what's for supper?' he asked.

You were looking straight at him. 'Saliva,' you replied.

'Ugh,' he grimaced.

'No,' I said, still ignoring our boy, and then smiling at him with the onslaught of inspiration. 'It's tartar.'

'I've never had tartar, do I like it?' he asked.

'Don't you see? It's salt repeatedly, that means two sailors, and tartar is dental trouble.'

Our boy was looking worried. 'Do you think I could just have tinned spaghetti with sausages?' he said, and for the first time of the day, we laughed together.

It always takes something silly like that to break the tension. And here we are now, in the bath, on equal pegging and just a few hands left to play. There is an unspoken prize to be won, to be presented, with the lights off, later still in bed. Win or lose you will make the tea and roll the joint that we will smoke as soon as this game is over and we are propped against our pillows watching something mind-numbing on the television. You deal the cards. I can't believe my luck. I get the ace, King, Queen and Jack of hearts, and hearts are trumps. You flick your fingers on the surface of the water, which makes a satisfyingly loud 'chlock'. The warm water laps against my shoulders, the light ripples dance above us. There is nowhere else I would rather be. There is no one else I would rather be with. I lie back and look at you through my soggy fan of trumps and manage to tell you for the first time today: 'Do you know,' I say, 'I'm lucky. I'm really so very lucky.'